REGINA RODGERS

The Long Ride to Love

by Regina Rodgers

ISBN-13: 978-1-959788-97-3

Acknowledgments: to my old buddy, Lewis Klaber, for his

creative assistance, brainstorming, and a really great title.

Chapter One

Late June 1869
Arizona Territory

Rusty Cunningham jolted awake. He lay motionless for a minute and listened. Something was out there near the herd. Maybe a coyote—he'd seen tracks earlier. The horses stamped and blew, nervous. If they stampeded, it might take days to round them up again.

He slid out of his bedroll and snatched his rifle. Crouching low, he crept toward the herd and circled around them to the edge of the water hole. There was movement near a copse of trees where the new stallions rested separate from the rest of the herd. He squatted next to a piñon tree and waited. Long ago, he'd learned that patience could mean survival. A rumble of low voices prompted him to lever a cartridge into his Spencer. He stayed still, not willing to expose his position and unsure how many men he'd have to deal with. Rusty's eyes adjusted to the desert starlight, and his peripheral vision caught the form of a man bent low and coming toward him. It was his trail boss, Jared Gentry.

A horse whinnied and reared. Raspy voices whispered to each other in rapid Spanish. Rusty could make out the forms of men leading Jared's horses from the herd and leaving others in their places.

Jared crawled in close to Rusty and raised his rifle. "They're swapping out my stallions."

Rusty grabbed Jared's arm. "Hold on. We need to wait for them to leave the herd. We can't risk hitting a horse or causing a stampede."

Jared nodded his agreement.

One thief gave a low whistle. Another led Jared's two prized stud horses from the herd and over to the piñon trees where their mounts waited, tethered. They saddled up, then one man shouted, "*Andale!*"

"They're not getting my stallions." Jared raised from his position next to Rusty and took off toward the men at a dead run.

"Jared, wait!" Rusty shouted, but it was too late.

Before Rusty could make a move, a pistol shot rang out and his boss fell to the ground. Jared's men came running from the campsite, shouting. The two thieving *vaqueros* spurred their horses and bolted.

Rusty dashed to his boss's side and dropped to his

knees. Jared clenched his hand to his chest, blood oozing from a bullet hole.

Without hesitation, several of Jared's men mounted up and chased the thieves south toward the Mexican border.

"Hold on, buddy, I'm going to get you some help." Rusty hoisted Jared over his shoulder and carried him to the campsite. He laid the injured man on his bedroll.

Jared grimaced. "Get my stallions back, Rusty. I can't lose those horses."

"I'm riding for help now. Just hold on…I'll be back as fast as I can." Rusty squeezed Jared's arm and left his side.

~

Sonora, Mexico
Earlier that evening

Rachel Del Carmen Rios bustled onto the shaded patio of Rancho del Rios. She seated herself on the edge of a round, blue-tiled fountain that dominated the terracotta court. Late afternoon sun glinted off the white stucco walls of the great adobe structure. From the west, a scorching desert wind gusted, sending a delicious, cool mist of water across her face. This was her favorite spot on the hacienda. A shady oasis where she could hide from the flurry of last-minute preparations taking place inside. And from her father. He and Tía Maria had spent weeks planning for tonight, but Rachel dreaded it with everything in herself.

Servants set up torches around the courtyard at the back of the hacienda and spread tables with plates, silverware, and crystal goblets. Inside, wrought-iron chandeliers glowed with dozens of candles. Deep-set windows and doors on both sides of the great room were open to allow a cross breeze.

Anxiety welled up inside Rachel. Tonight, her father would stand before their friends and neighbors and announce her engagement to Paulo Delgado. On what should have been one of the happiest days of her young life, sadness engulfed her. Instead of viewing tonight as a joyful beginning, it felt like an unhappy ending.

Rachel's shoulders tensed as she recalled the angry words she'd had with Papá earlier. She'd told him more than once that she didn't want to marry Paulo, but her objections fell on deaf ears. She could hear his reply in her mind even now. *"This is what is best for you, my daughter. You will learn to love Paulo."*

The iron gate creaked open, and Rachel looked up, quickly pasting on a smile. Paulo strode across the tiled patio toward her, a brilliant smile on his arrogant face. He made a slight bow and took her extended hand, brushing her fingers with his lips.

"My dear, how lovely you look this evening," he said. "The loveliest flower in this garden."

"Thank you, Paulo." She gave a weak smile.

"You're early, aren't you?" She gestured to her maid. "Bonita, please bring Señor Delgado a glass of something cold."

Paulo sat next to Rachel and removed his black, flat-topped hat. As always, dressed to perfection, Paulo cut a dashing figure in his elaborately decorated, snug-fitting pants and short *charro* jacket. His hatband, studded with silver conchos, caught the last rays of the sun. He was a handsome man, with his snapping black eyes, thick, wavy hair, and a pencil-thin mustache. In Rachel's opinion, the only problem was that *he* was much too aware of that fact. It was only one aspect of Paulo's personality that left her cold.

"Why are you here early?" she asked again as Bonita brought his drink on a silver serving tray.

Paulo shrugged. "I was eager to see you. I hope you don't mind that I'm here ahead of the other guests." He moved closer beside her and put a hand on her bare arm. She instinctively recoiled at his touch. His hands were soft and smooth. Hands that had never known a day of labor and, she was sure, never would.

"No, not at all, Paulo." She laughed lightly and inched away from him. "It will be a beautiful party. Tía Maria and my sisters have spent days preparing for this *fiesta* and all day today setting things up. Neighbors from everywhere will be arriving soon. It should be a wonderful evening."

He scooted closer to her again and wrapped an arm around her waist. "Yes, a wonderful evening. In a few weeks, we'll have the biggest, most elaborate wedding anyone in this territory has seen in decades." He laughed and looked up at the giant palm trees shading the patio. "You and I will be Sonora's most beautiful and influential couple." He moved to kiss her, but she turned her head. His lips only grazed her cheek.

Paulo stiffened and cast a tense look at her. "This shyness of yours is most endearing, but it must come to an end soon, my sweet Rachel." His smile tightened as he released her from his embrace.

"I'm sorry, Paulo—you're right. I'm sure I'll overcome my shyness by the time we're wed." But it was a lie. She'd never welcome his embrace. While she didn't despise Paulo, she didn't love him. She knew he wasn't the man she wanted to wake up next to for the next fifty years.

Another breeze sent a spray of cool mist from the fountain across the two of them. Rachel smiled and turned her face into it, but Paulo jumped up and furiously wiped the moisture from the front of his expensive silk shirt.

"Really, Rachel! Do you enjoy this sort of foolishness?" His voice was rough with irritation.

She couldn't help but laugh. "Paulo, do you never enjoy the little things of life?" She could only shake her head at him. "Come on, I think I hear people gathering inside." She picked up her lemonade and took his arm. "Let's go in and let Papá know you're here."

Rachel strolled into the great room and saw her father, Domingo Rios, standing amongst three other men, talking local politics, as usual. He looked up and smiled broadly as they approached. "Here's the happy young couple now. Come, my daughter, let us toast you and your handsome husband-to-be!"

"Yes, son, come! Let us raise a glass to the young couple who represents the joining of two great families." Paulo's father, Enrique Delgado clapped a hand on his son's shoulder and drew him into the small group of men. Rachel's father and a wealthy neighbor, Juan Rodriguez, also raised their goblets.

She lifted her glass of lemonade. "But Papá, the guests are only beginning to arrive. Shouldn't we wait?"

"Oh, this will be only the first of many toasts to your happiness," Domingo said.

Rachel pasted a smile on her face. *Ha! What does my happiness have to do with it? This wedding is only about the merging of two wealthy families.*

"To Paulo and Rachel. May they have a lifetime of happiness and many children to comfort their old age."

The three men raised their glasses toward the young couple. "To Paulo and Rachel!"

"Thank you, everyone." She smiled at the group of men. "Now, I really should help Tía Maria greet our guests." She excused herself and swept across the room to her aunt and younger sisters, Teresa and Ana, who welcomed their arriving guests. The mariachi musicians began to play. Their joyful music drifted in from the courtyard, a signal that the fiesta had begun.

~

Rachel stood beside her aunt and sisters, greeting guests as they entered the fiesta.

Paulo approached the group of women and handed Rachel a glass of Madeira. She frowned. "Paulo, you know I don't drink alcohol."

"Oh, come, my dear. You're a grown woman, and we're celebrating our engagement. Surely you can share one glass of wine with me." Rachel accepted the glass but didn't put it to her lips.

Teresa rolled her eyes. "Yes, Rachel. You're eighteen years old and still refusing a glass of wine." She smiled at Paulo and tilted her head. "Were I engaged to such a handsome and distinguished man, I assure you I'd be drinking wine with him and dancing in his arms." She gazed at Paulo from under thick lashes, not attempting to hide her admiration.

Tía Maria and Ana gasped at Teresa's brazen statement, but Rachel merely smiled. A hint of irritation crept into her voice. "Please, Teresa. You *should* dance with your future brother-in-law and have your fill of wine. As Paulo said, it is a celebration."

Eleven-year-old Ana wrinkled her nose in distaste. "What's so special about getting married, anyway? Once you're married, you can't have any more fun."

Tía Maria coughed, dabbed her nose with a handkerchief, and looked away. Teresa rolled her eyes at her younger sibling.

Paulo merely shook his head at the girl, then bowed to the group of women. "Please excuse us." He took Rachel by the hand and led her out onto the patio. "Dance with me, *querida*," he said. He pulled her close and put his lips to her ear. "Soon, I'll be free to show you how strong my love for you truly is."

Rachel pulled away from him, feeling something close to repulsion. "I'm sorry, Paulo. There's something I forgot to tell Papá. I must go speak to him."

She flew away from Paulo and ran into the courtyard where the crowd of guests milled, danced, and enjoyed the food and music, leaving Paulo standing alone, staring after her.

Rachel forced herself to look happy as she hurried to her father's side. He stood as she came near and held out his hand to her. "My dear, is something wrong? Why aren't you inside with Paulo?"

Her breath was shallow after her sprint from the patio. "Nothing is wrong, Papá. I simply wanted to spend some time here with you and our guests." She took him by the hand and pulled him to a bench at the edge of the torch-lit courtyard.

Domingo sat his squat body on the bench beside her and straightened his embroidered charro jacket. "Alright, my daughter." He looked into her eyes. "Tell me what's troubling you. You can't fool me, *mija*.

Aren't you happy with the fiesta your Papá has given you?"

"Yes, of course, I am." She squeezed his hand and exhaled slowly, not wanting to tell him the truth—that the man he'd selected to be her husband was a silly and repugnant peacock in her eyes. That every time he was in their home, he was visually appraising the contents.

Papá turned her face to him. "I know you, my daughter. Something is bothering you. You aren't happy tonight."

Rachel turned away. "You know what it is, Papá. I've already told you. I don't love Paulo. I don't *want* to be married to him." She scrunched her face in distaste.

He frowned. "What is this? Paulo is the most suitable young man in Sonora for you."

"Don't you understand? I want to have a marriage like the one you and Mamá shared. One filled with love and devotion." Rachel's voice broke, hoarse and miserable.

Domingo took her chin in his hand. "My dear. Love will grow. The marriage between your mother and me was an arranged one, but in a short time, we grew to love each other completely." He patted her hand. "You must trust that the same will be true for you and Paulo. Believe me—this is what's best for you."

She shook her head and mentioned another truth. "And I miss Mamá." Tears threatened to spill over. Even though Paulo was the immediate cause of her distress, her mother was heavy on her mind.

She looked around her at the dancing guests. "You and Tía Maria have done such a wonderful job of preparing this fiesta, but I can't help but think how happy it would have made Mamá. How she would have been in the center of this courtyard whirling and dancing the *fandango*. How she would have been at my side helping me choose my dress and jewelry for this evening." Tears finally overflowed and trailed down her cheeks.

Papá drew Rachel close to his side, a tear of his own threatening to track down his sun-weathered face. "Yes, my daughter. I should have known this. I should have been aware. Your Tía Maria has taken so much of this task upon herself that I haven't been as thoughtful of your feelings as I should have." He released his tight grip on her shoulders. "And I didn't want to trouble you with my sadness. Your Mamá has been on my mind, too, during this time. Her face has been in my memory constantly as I've prepared for our eldest daughter's marriage."

"Oh, Papá, forgive me for burdening you with this."

He kissed her cheek. "No, no, my dear, it's no burden. On the contrary, it is only natural the two of us should think of your Mamá at this time. Perhaps we should take comfort in our shared memories of her."

"Yes, Papá, you're right."

~

Rachel looked up and saw Paulo cross the

courtyard, his stride purposeful and eyes angry. She hoped he wouldn't confront her about leaving him alone on the patio. But it wasn't his words that broke the silence.

Pounding hoof beats neared the courtyard. A small group of riders burst through the open gate of the sprawling hacienda, horses rearing as the men reined in sharply. The man who appeared to be in charge slid from the back of his tall mount. "I'm told there's a doctor here. And I need to speak with Delgado."

Rachel stood and broke free from her father's protective grasp. This man wasn't like any Americano she'd ever seen. He towered over Paulo, who had moved forward when the stranger mentioned the Delgado name. The cowboy's hat hung down his back on a leather lanyard, revealing a shock of thick, auburn hair. He was broad-shouldered with a slender but powerful build. Not what most would call handsome by any means, but with a strong, distinctive face.

"Are you Delgado?" he asked.

"I am Paulo Delgado. Is it me you want or my father, Enrique Delgado?"

"I'm looking for the man who owns the spread near here. The man who sold my boss, Jared Gentry, a herd of mustangs and two stud stallions yesterday." He stepped in close to Paulo. His voice was deep and commanding. "Is that you?" He looked down at the smaller man through narrowed eyes.

Before Paulo could answer, Enrique strode up to

the cowboy. "I'm Señor Delgado. And who might you be?"

"The name's Rusty Cunningham." He leveled a withering glare at Delgado. "Jared Gentry's waiting north of here, shot in the chest. A couple of vaqueros tried to steal two breeding stallions from our herd and replace them with some inferior stock. Our men caught them before they got a quarter of a mile away." He inched closer to Delgado. "They both claimed they worked for you."

Señor Delgado's eyebrows shot up. "What? This can't be!" Murmurs broke out in the crowd.

"Well, sir, it *can* be, and I'm telling you, it happened. Now, where is that doctor, if you've got one here? I need to get him to Gentry right now."

A distinguished-looking man with graying hair stepped forward into the torchlight. "I'm Dr. Garcia. Take me to this injured man. I'll do what I can for him."

"Alright, Doc, let's go." He turned to Enrique Delgado. "Oh, and you ought to know that we've got them two vaqueros of yours tied up and waiting for the *rurales*. Maybe you'd like to come along and deal with them yourself. I know for sure what we'd do with them where I come from back in Tennessee." He remounted his horse and swept the group with his eyes. They rested an extra moment on Rachel. "Ma'am." He nodded to her and rode out of the courtyard.

~

Rusty's horse pounded its way toward the campsite where he'd left his friend Jared Gentry. Enrique Delgado rode with Dr. Garcia in his buggy, and several of Delgado's men followed on horseback. Rusty half expected to see those horse thieves hang tonight, and it wouldn't bother him much if it happened. The only thing that concerned him was getting that bullet removed from Jared's chest. He whispered a prayer that he'd still be alive when they got there.

Ten miles north of the ranchero, Rusty reigned in and led Dr. Garcia to Jared.

"Hold a lantern for me." Dr. Garcia removed the temporary bandaging someone had applied to the wound and gave a cursory examination. He turned to Rusty. "The bullet doesn't seem to have hit any major organ, but he does have a broken rib." The doctor wiped blood from his hands. "I suggest we transport him back to the Rios hacienda and let me operate in a clean bed with good lighting, where I can better see what I'm doing."

"Yes, of course, Doc." Rusty agreed without hesitation. "If he ain't in danger of bleeding to death, and you think it best, let's get him back to the Rios spread."

Rusty and one of his men lifted Jared into the back of a wagon and headed toward the hacienda. He shouted to Señor Delgado. "How are you going to deal with these horse thieves? Like I said, it's totally up to you."

"We'll take them with us back to my *ranchero*. When the rurales are through with them, they will probably wish we'd hanged them."

~

An hour later, Rachel watched the group of men ride through the gates of the Rios hacienda. Her papá directed the men to take Jared to one of the spare bedrooms. Rusty and Dr. Garcia followed behind.

Rachel raced up the staircase behind the men to the guest room, where they laid Jared out on the bed. "Doctor, what can I do to help?"

"Get me another lamp and some boiling water. And tear up a clean sheet for bandages," he said.

Rachel hurried from the room and gathered the requested supplies. A short time later, Jared Gentry rested comfortably while Rusty hovered nearby.

Dr. Garcia washed his hands and closed his medical bag. "I'll be back early tomorrow to check on my patient."

Rachel helped the doctor into his jacket. "Is there anything I need to do for him until you return?"

"Give him a teaspoon of this for pain every few hours." He handed her an amber-colored bottle of liquid. "And give him plenty of beef broth to help rebuild the blood he's lost."

He walked to the door. "I'll see you tomorrow."

Rachel turned her eyes on the cowboy who hadn't moved from his boss's side since entering the hacienda.

"Come with me. Señor Gentry is sleeping soundly, and you should eat something. How long has it been since you've had food? I'm sure the cook has some fresh tortillas and beef to fill them."

Rusty looked up at her, uncertainty in his hazel-green eyes. "Well, I don't remember for sure. I reckon it's been a while. But I can't leave Jared."

"Come." She gestured toward the door. "I'll have my maid, Bonita, sit with him. She will alert us if he wakes up." She led Rusty down the stairs and across the great room, still filled with the last vestiges of her engagement fiesta.

Paulo stepped from the shadows. "I see that you ruined our evening only to turn this home into a hospital for gringo cowboys. Is that correct, my dear?" His voice dripped with anger and sarcasm.

Startled, Rachel stopped in her tracks and whirled around to look at him. "You're still here, Paulo? I thought you had gone home." Beside her, Rusty slowly turned his gaze on the man.

Paulo shifted his eyes from Rachel to the cowboy. "Yes, I'm still here. And who is this?" He glared at Rusty.

"Of course, I'm sorry. Paulo, this is—" Suddenly, she realized that she couldn't remember Rusty's last name. She looked at him, embarrassed.

"That's okay, ma'am. My name is Cunningham— Nathaniel Cunningham. Most people call me Rusty."

Paulo didn't respond, and Rachel narrowed her

eyes at him. "This is Paulo Delgado. I believe you two met earlier in the courtyard when you came to get Dr. Garcia." Somehow, she couldn't bring herself to introduce Paulo as her fiancé.

Rusty gave a short laugh. "Sure. How could I forget? I took your pa with me to the campsite where my boss laid shot and bleeding at the hands of his vaqueros." He stepped closer to Paulo. "I hope it's okay with you if he rests here until he heals enough to ride. And right now, I wouldn't trust him in the hands of anybody on the Delgado ranch, anyway."

Paulo's face grew dark and ugly with anger. "You would be well-advised to take care how you speak of my family, Señor. Don't forget you are a visitor here amongst us."

Rusty shifted his weight casually to one foot and cocked an eyebrow, displaying all the fear and concern he would have shown an unruly child.

"And *you'd* be well-advised to remember that Jared Gentry came here to buy a herd from your father, and what he got was robbed and shot by some of your men. Although we've had no apology for that, I ain't exactly holding it against your pa." He fixed Paulo with a hard look. "And you'd be wise to remember that I'll be watching over my friend until he's well enough to leave for home. So don't be throwing any threats my way that you ain't prepared to back up."

He turned back to Rachel. "Ma'am. I think I could eat a bite of supper, after all."

Chapter Two

Rusty awoke to rain hitting the bedroom window—a rare but much-welcomed event after the previous day's heat. A night on the floor had left his back stiff, and he stretched, then shoved his pallet of quilts aside. Going straight to Jared, he checked for fever and found that his skin was cool to the touch.

Jared's eyes flickered open. He looked around in confusion, then tried to raise himself. He groaned in pain. Rusty gently pushed him back onto the pillow. "Easy there, Jared. You've been shot. Lay back down. You ain't going anywhere."

"Shot?" Jared put a hand to his forehead and rubbed it as if he could will his memory to work.

Rusty pulled a chair up to the bed and sat down. "Yes, shot. It's a bit of a story—"

A knock sounded at the door. It opened, and Bonita walked in carrying a tray of something that smelled wonderful. Rachel followed with a pitcher of fresh water and a roll of bandages. It might have been raining outside, but sunshine had just walked through the door.

"Good morning, gentlemen."

A warm smile lit Rachel's face. She wore a full red skirt and a ruffled yellow blouse. Her sleek, shiny, black hair was pulled back in a twist. Her olive skin was smooth and flawless. She was one of the prettiest things Rusty had ever seen. Maybe the prettiest.

Rachel pulled open the drapes that covered the deep-set window and put her water pitcher and bandages on the table next to Jared. "How do you feel this morning, Señor Gentry?"

"He don't seem to have a fever," Rusty leaned forward in the chair and rested his elbows on his knees.

Rachel brushed aside Jared's dark hair and touched his brow then sat down next to the bed. "No, you're right, he does not." She turned back to Jared. "Dr. Garcia will be here today, but I want to look at your wound and change the bandage this morning."

Rachel picked up the bowl from the tray. "Bonita has brought you some beef broth and tortillas. Would you like to have a little food before I give you your pain medicine? I remember my Papá saying it was easier on his stomach if he ate first."

"Thank you, ma'am," Jared said, finally able to speak for himself. "If Rusty could help me sit up, I'd try a bit of coffee."

Rusty raised from his chair and gently took him by one arm while Rachel took hold of the other. Between the two of them, they eased Jared into an upright position. The scent of her clean hair wafted to Rusty's nostrils as she plumped Jared's pillows and propped them behind his back.

Sweat broke out on Jared's brow.

"I know you're in great pain. You were shot in the chest, and the doctor says you have a broken rib," she said.

Jared laid a hand on his chest. "I sure do feel that broken rib."

Rachel poured him a cup of strong-smelling coffee and lifted the mug to his lips. He sipped it and then let his head drop back against the pillow behind him.

She picked up a tortilla, rolled it up, and dipped it in the beef broth. "Here. Try to get a few bites of this down. You need to take your pain medication." Jared raised his head again and gave her a grateful look.

Rachel dismissed her maid. "Thank you, Bonita. Señor Rusty and I will be down soon to have our breakfast." Bonita nodded and closed the door behind herself.

"Oh, no—that ain't necessary for me." Rusty shook his head. "I can just eat a couple of these tortillas and then check on the herd."

"Nonsense, you need a good meal. Our cook has prepared a wonderful breakfast for everyone."

Jared sipped his coffee. "Well, one thing is sure. Somebody needs to tell me what happened yesterday. I must've lost consciousness for a while. And, by the way, exactly where am I?"

Rusty took a deep breath and set about explaining what had happened at the campsite the evening before and how Delgado's men had tried to switch out the stud stallions for lesser quality horses. "The Doc had us bring you back here to Señor Rios' place." He angled his head toward Rachel. "That's Miss Rios. She's been taking good care of you since we brought you here." He smiled at her.

Jared nodded. "I sure do thank you, ma'am."

"You are most welcome. My family and I will do all we can to make you comfortable while you're here." She spooned beef broth into his mouth. "I'm sure my father will be in to see you as soon as you feel up to talking to him."

"I don't expect to be here for more than a day or two. We still have a herd of horses to get into Tucson."

Rusty gave a short laugh. "You ain't gonna be going anywhere in a couple of days. Do you want to bleed to death? You're weak as a kitten now, anyway. We've got a fine bunch of wranglers to get that herd into Tucson. Just get that idea right out of your head."

There was a knock at the door, and at Rachel's prompt, Dr. Garcia entered.

Rusty nodded to the doctor and said to Jared, "I'll be back to check in with you before long. I'm heading out to the campsite to see how things are there. I reckon you'll want them to start the herd for Tucson right away."

"That's right," Jared answered. "Get them moving, Rusty. As a matter of fact, I'd feel a lot better if you'd go with them."

"No, Dave Fletcher is a good man—he can ramrod the drive till I can join back up with them. I'll be back here later today." Rusty grabbed a couple of tortillas from the stack on Jared's plate. He strode across the floor, closed the door, and left, brooking no argument from his boss, Jared Gentry.

Chapter Three

Rachel listened to Dr. Garcia's instructions for Jared's continued care and bid him good day. She excused herself and left him to examine his patient.

As Rachel reached the bottom of the stairs, she saw Tía Maria striding across the vast dining room like a general marching into battle. Bonita trotted along behind in a futile attempt to keep up. Her aunt twisted the fan in her hands and then tapped it rapidly in her palm when she reached her niece.

"Rachel, did you not know that your fiancé was to be here first thing this morning? Paulo is waiting for you in the great room."

"What? Surely not, Tía. Why would he be here so early this morning?"

"I don't know, *sobrina*. I suggest you go and find out. He will be your husband soon. You must learn how to keep him mollified. Life is not happy for a woman with an angry husband."

Rachel looked toward the patio. "Then I fear that my life will never be happy because Paulo is always angry." She turned to Bonita. "Please go up and sit with Señor Gentry. He was awake when I came downstairs."

"I will sit with him for a while." Tía Maria sounded determined. "I'd like to learn more about this man we have recovering in our home." She frowned. "How do we know we can trust this stranger? Maybe we should post a guard outside his door."

Rachel couldn't help but roll her eyes. "Tía, the man is in no shape to do any harm, but do what you think best. I must go find out what has Paulo agitated at this hour of the morning."

Paulo paced back and forth near the massive oak doors as he waited for Rachel. The sound of rain splashing on the patio, and the scent of creosote and sagebrush drifted through the open doors. When Rachel entered the room, a clap of thunder startled her. She walked past Paulo and gazed outside, beyond the gates, and into the desert. Lightning flashed, followed by another rumble of thunder. The tall American cowboy was riding through this downpour. Did he have his slicker with him? Surely, he must.

She turned to Paulo. He made a curt bow, his face twisted in anger.

"Yes, Paulo? I'm surprised to see you here so early this morning—and in the midst of a storm." Rachel steeled herself against the torrent of angry words she knew were about to bombard her. "You seem upset. Is something wrong?"

Paulo threw his hands up in exasperation and

tossed his hat onto a carved mahogany chair. "Surely, you jest, Rachel. You must know why I'm here this morning and why I'm angry." He turned and continued to pace the distance from one end of the carpet to the other. "Last night was our engagement fiesta." He gestured wildly in his anger. "All our neighbors were here to celebrate with us. And not only did you leave the party to play nursemaid to the *Americano,* but you spent the last part of the evening feeding supper to that—gringo cowboy. You ignored our guests and—and me!" He stopped pacing and came to her, putting his hands on her shoulders. Rachel stiffened under his touch.

"And this, Rachel." He tightened his grip, his voice low and frustrated. "Why do you treat me as though I were the village ogre?"

Rachel turned her head away from him. "Don't be ridiculous, Paulo. I do no such thing." He pulled her face to him and glared into her eyes. He sighed and then released her.

Rachel walked back to the open doors and stared out into the rain. "What would you have had me do? Señor Gentry came here wounded, and we didn't know how badly. A man's life was at stake."

"There were many others here to help the wounded Americano. There was no need for you to abandon our guests."

Rachel turned to him. "Perhaps I didn't handle things as well as I should have, but the evening was already well spent when the American cowboys arrived here with Dr. Garcia."

Paulo returned to her side. "I will speak to your papá about these things, my dear. I'll expect to see some changes in your behavior before our wedding day. You need to learn your place in this relationship." Paulo spun on his heel and stormed out of the room.

Rachel watched him go and then turned back to gaze out the open doors. *Hmph. Learn my place, indeed. I may not know where my place is yet, but I know it's not with you, Paulo Delgado.*

She followed him out the door of the great room. The staccato sound of his boots tromping across the floor echoed in the foyer. She looked up and saw a slender figure at the top of the stairs. Her sister glided down the grand staircase as though her feet didn't touch the ground. Paulo stopped just as she reached the bottom of the steps.

"You're leaving so soon, Paulo?" Teresa smiled and extended her hand to him. She flushed at the touch of his lips on her fingers.

"Yes, I needed to discuss a small matter with Rachel." He glanced back at her. "Forgive me, I must be on my way. I have some rather urgent business to take care of this morning." He nodded to Teresa as he turned. "It was a pleasure to see you. I wish my visit could have been so pleasant with everyone."

"Señor Delgado." Teresa's eyes rested softly on him. "I hope to see you again soon."

~

Rusty crested the rise overlooking Jared Gentry's herd of horses and reined in his tall roan, Copper. The rain had stopped, at least for now, and the sun broke through the clouds. The rainy season was upon them, and unfortunately, the downpour could start again at any time. He began his descent into the camp. He'd update the men on Jared's condition and tell Dave Fletcher to get the herd on its way to Tucson.

Rusty made his way into camp, rode up to Dave, and nodded hello.

"How about a cup of coffee, Cunningham?"

"Don't mind if I do." He accepted the cup Dave offered and sat down on a water barrel in the shade of the chuck wagon. "Jared's doing okay," he said, getting right to the point. "He's on the mend—shot below the shoulder, and Doc says it didn't hit anything that'll kill him unless he gets an infection. He has a busted rib, though."

Dave raised his eyebrows. "Well, that's some good news. I don't mind telling you that I was scared when he took a bullet last night. I suppose somebody's dealt with those vaqueros?"

Rusty shrugged and took another swallow of coffee. "I can't say for sure, but Delgado said he'd turn them over to the rurales. I plan to follow up with him to make sure that happens."

Dave agreed. "Glad to hear you say that."

Rusty scanned the herd of two hundred horses.

"That's a beautiful herd there, and them two studs are some of the finest I've ever seen." He squinted at the reflection of something up in the crest he'd just ridden down from. "Dave, you and the men go on ahead and drive the herd up to Tucson. You take the lead and ramrod this outfit. Buy the supplies you need and get the herd started for the Shawnee trail in Texas. You know what you're doing."

He looked up toward the ridge again. His eyes settled on a horse-mounted figure. "You've got company up there, Dave." He raised his eyes to the crest. "I'm going to try to check it out, but if he runs before I get there, you and the men stay alert. I'm betting that's one of Delgado's men nosing around."

Dave put a hand on his sidearm. "I see him. I'll let the boys know to keep their eyes open. We don't want another man wounded."

Rusty stood and set his coffee cup on top of the barrel. "Okay, Dave. You get this outfit moving, and you'd best put out point men and flankers now that we know you're being watched."

"You can count on it."

The men shook hands, and Rusty mounted up. *Who is on that ridge watching the herd?*

Rusty made a point of not looking up toward the crest. He rode out of the campsite at an unhurried pace. Once he reached the shelter of a line of juniper trees, he lashed his horse with the reins and made his way up the ridge as fast as possible without sliding on the loose rock.

Whoever was up on the crest would have made tracks as soon as he noticed Rusty leaving the camp.

When he neared the top, he slowed down and took his time, making no sudden moves to attract attention to himself. The watcher might still be around. Rusty sat in the shade of the trees for a minute. Then, from the corner of his eye, he glimpsed the pale tail of a palomino disappearing over the summit of the trail.

A palomino. Paulo had been riding one last night when he was at the hacienda. And he remembered Paulo's silver belt buckle and concho hatband. Suddenly, Paulo Delgado seemed a likely suspect. Rusty got back on the trail and headed for the Rancho del Rios.

~

Rusty took the steps of the wide staircase three at a time. He needed to check on Jared and tell him about the mysterious observer he'd seen near the campsite. As he reached the top of the stairs, the door opened, and he was surprised to see an elegant woman come through the door. She stopped in her tracks and waited. Her bearing was regal as she folded her hands and waited for him to reach her.

Rusty stopped and removed his hat. "You're Miss Rachel's aunt, aren't you?"

"*Sí*, I'm Señora Rios, sister to Rachel's papá. May I help you?"

"Yes, ma'am. I was with Mr. Gentry when we brought him here wounded last night." Rusty fidgeted with his hat. "I need to talk to him if he's awake. He'll want a report on his herd."

She dipped her head. "He is awake and resting. I just spent a short time talking with him. I suggest that you don't tire him out with worry about his herd of horses."

Rusty widened his eyes in surprise at her commanding tone. "Yes, ma'am. I'll make it a quick visit."

She stepped aside and allowed him to enter the bedroom.

Rusty closed the door behind himself and smiled when he saw Jared propped up against two pillows and alert. He pulled a velvet-covered armchair to the bedside and sat down. "Well, I'm glad to see you awake. You're looking pretty danged good for a man that was just shot in the chest last night." Rusty's grin spread from ear to ear.

Jared sounded drowsy but strong. "Yeah, I guess I'm gonna live," he said, only half in jest. "But before I fall asleep again after taking that pain medicine, there's something important I need you to do."

"Sure, Jared. Name it.'

His eyes met Rusty's. "Get word to Evangeline. Let her know what's happened with me and the herd. Tell her that Dave Fletcher will be bringing the horses in without me." He looked toward the window. "She'll be worried but let her know that I'll only be a week or two behind."

Rusty reached over and squeezed his friend's arm. "You bet I will."

Jared gave a weak laugh. "She'll be waiting and

watching to see us ride into Independence.”

“Don’t worry about a thing. I’ll telegraph her.” He sat back in the chair. “I talked to Dave. He’s gonna get the herd started north. Him and a couple of men will go on into Tucson and stock up on fresh supplies. Then they’ll get the herd moving toward Texas and hook up to the Shawnee trail.”

“Thank you, buddy. It sounds like you’ve got things under control.” He reached out his hand and Rusty gripped it. Then, before he could say another word, Jared’s head dropped. He was sound asleep. Rusty sighed. He’d have to wait to tell Jared about the mysterious man on the ridge.

~

Intent on cutting a few flowers for the great room, Rachel strolled onto the back patio. Loud whoops and excited shouts of vaqueros sitting around the small corral assailed her ears. She turned toward the commotion and held a hand up to shade her eyes. The American cowboy strode toward the paddock, his saddle hefted over one broad shoulder. His long legs ate the distance from the tack room to the corral in a few short strides.

Dropping her shears and basket, Rachel dashed to the fence. The vaqueros yelling continued. “Stay on him, Pedro—you can do it!”

Rusty dropped his saddle to the ground beside him and climbed the fence. He took a seat on the top rail, watching the cowboy attempt to ride the untamed mustang.

"Hang in there, Pedro!" The vaquero next to him cupped his hands around his mouth and yelled.

Pedro held the reins of the bucking bronco in his left hand and raised his free arm high in the air. The mustang bucked and thrashed, circling round and round the corral. After a few more seconds, Pedro flew over the horse's head and landed flat on his back. He lay still for a moment, then stood up, grabbed his sombrero and whacked it against his chaps, dust flying everywhere. "You evil horse, no man could ride you." He limped toward the fence, then turned back to the horse. "I will ride you, devil horse!" he shouted.

The vaqueros howled and playfully taunted. "Nice try, Pedro."

Rusty shoved his Stetson back and laughed along with the men.

Rachel climbed onto the lowest rail of the fence and stood beside him. She flashed a smile. "Pedro is usually one of Papá's best horse trainers but I see he's having some difficulty today." She giggled as Pedro fussed and fumed at the horse.

"We don't call him Diablo for no reason." Pedro removed his sombrero and swiped sweat from his forehead with his sleeve.

Rusty looked out at Diablo in the corral, then at Pedro. "Are you trying to saddle break him?"

"Yes, more men than me have tried but no one has been able to stay on his back until he stops bucking and starts walking."

Rusty stared at the ground for a moment and then looked at Pedro. He raised an eyebrow. "Have you ever tried riding him in water?"

Pedro stopped coiling the rope he held and eyed Rusty suspiciously. "In the water?"

Rachel turned and focused her attention on Rusty.

"Yeah. A couple of years back I worked with an Arapaho man. He taught me to break a horse the way his people do it—take him into some deep water and let him wear himself out."

Pedro's eyes widened and then he blurted out a short laugh.

Rachel turned to Rusty. "We have a deep pond just over in that grove of trees. Can you show us how to do this horse breaking in the pond?"

"Well, I reckon I can give it a try." He hopped down and strode toward Diablo. When he reached him, he stroked the stallion's neck and cooed to him softly. "Good fella. You and me are gonna be friends."

He made a clicking noise, took the horse's reins, and started leading him toward the gate Pedro had opened. "Come on, Diablo."

Rachel ran ahead and led the group of men and Diablo to the large pond she'd mentioned. She made a wide, sweeping motion toward the water. "Here you go, Señor Cunningham."

He led the stallion into the pond and slowly pulled him deeper into the water turning him in a large circle until Diablo adjusted to the feeling of being submerged up to his shoulders.

Rusty stroked the horse's side. "Come on, Diablo. You're the beast and I'm the man. The good Lord put me in charge of you." He slowly laid himself across the horse's back and allowed him to swim around the pond in a large circle. After several minutes had passed, he put a foot in the stirrup and climbed into the saddle. Diablo bucked and thrashed, furious at the man trying to force his will on him. He reared and fought, but with his body in the water, it had little effect. He tossed his head and whipped around until he exhausted himself and began to swim the perimeter of the huge pond.

Rusty's Stetson fell behind his shoulders, the bright sun gleaming a burnished sheen off his auburn hair.

Rachel watched in amazement. Entranced, she couldn't remove her eyes from the cowboy as he took command of Diablo. He was in his element. The self-assurance and strength he emanated was something she'd seen in no other man.

Finally, he led Diablo out of the water and circled the pond one time on dry ground. Diablo made a fuss and reared a couple of times, but he had the idea—he allowed Rusty to stay on his back. Rusty dismounted, led him back to the corral, and unsaddled him. He pulled a sugar cube from his shirt pocket and fed it to Diablo. "Good boy." He stroked his nose. "You're gonna make some lucky man a fine mount."

Pedro ambled up to Rusty's side. "Well, Señor, I

must give you credit. I have never seen anything like that. It was a pleasure to watch."

Rusty smiled and nodded. "That's all he needs for today. If you want me to, I'll show you the next step tomorrow, but for today, just let him alone." He picked up his saddle and started for the barn. "He's done a good day's work."

Rachel scurried up beside him and fell into step. She gazed at him and contemplated his face as they strolled into the barn.

"That was an amazing thing to watch. I'd say you've changed the way Papá's vaqueros will train the difficult horses forever."

He lifted the corner of his lip into a crooked smile. "It ain't that big of a thing once you know how to do it."

"Well, you certainly seem to know how. Your Arapaho friend taught you well. Nobody has been able to ride Diablo."

Rusty grabbed a brush and began working his way down his roan's back.

She leaned against a workbench, picked up a curry comb and ran her fingers across its teeth. "Where do you come from, Señor Cunningham? I'm curious about you."

He looked her way, quirking one brow above his hazel eyes.

"I'm from Tennessee, ma'am. But I've made my home in Missouri for the past couple of years. I really like it there—it's good horse country."

"Missouri must be a beautiful place."

He stopped brushing the horse and his face lit up. "Yes, it is." For a moment, his eyes appeared distant. "I have my sights set on a few hundred acres near Jared's ranch. When you top a rise, the miles just seem to roll before you, all green and kinda misty-looking. Of course, it'll take lots of hard work and more money in the bank, but good Lord willing, it will be mine within a few years."

His voice was soft and deep. It seemed to wrap itself around Rachel's heart and tug. Her skin tingled and she rubbed her arms.

Unbidden, an image formed in her mind. She rode next to this tall cowboy down a green Missouri hill dotted in the distance by horses and wildflowers. She shook it off. *Rachel, you just met this man.*

A young girl's voice rang out behind them making Rachel jump.

"Tía Maria is looking for you. She won't be happy if she finds out you're loitering here in the barn."

Rachel whipped around and hurried to Ana's side. "Well, then, don't tell her, little Miss Bossy."

Ana crossed her arms. "Humph. Maybe I will and maybe I won't." She flicked her eyes up to Rusty and gave him a dimpled smile. "Good morning, Señor."

He curled his lips into a crooked smile and winked at her.

Ana turned on her heels and fled from the barn.

Rachel paused at the door and then turned to Rusty, a smile lighting her face. "I hope you have a pleasant day, Señor Rusty."

Chapter Four

Nothing in Rusty's life had prepared him for the spectacle called breakfast in the Rios dining room. He'd grown up in a three-room cabin in the Cumberland Mountains of Tennessee. He and his ma, pa, and five siblings would all crowd down the length of a pine plank table at breakfast and supper. Pa would say grace and then start the orderly passing of bowls of biscuits and gravy at breakfast or a big pot of pinto beans and a plate of cornbread at supper. Heaven help any young'un that tried to grab food out of turn. He knew the rules for mealtimes back home, but this was a new experience.

Rusty was still taking his meals with Jared in his sick room a week after he'd arrived wounded at the Rios' hacienda. But this morning, Rachel had insisted that Rusty come down and eat with the family. He'd run out of excuses to say no.

Despite feeling like a fish out of water, Rusty relented. He shaved, combed his hair, and tucked his best wrinkled shirt into the waist of his trousers. He rubbed the toe of each boot on the back of a pant leg and started downstairs like a man on the way to his own hanging. When he reached the dining room door, Rachel stood and hurried over to greet him.

"Señor Rusty, please come in and join us." She took his arm and led him into the room. Rusty's nerves tingled as she led him past the stern eyes of her Papá, Tía Maria, and Teresa, and the curious eyes of young Ana. Rusty had no fear of facing down a horse rustler or climbing onto the back of an unbroken mustang stallion, but walking into this dining room intimidated him. His every instinct told him he didn't belong here, but Rachel had such a firm grasp on him that he couldn't have left her side if he'd tried.

She led him to the enormous buffet on the far side of the dining room. "I've waited to fill my plate, in case you are not familiar with some of our foods." Mouth-watering aromas teased his nostrils as he neared the selection of dishes. Rachel picked up a plate from a stack at one end of the sideboard and made her way down the buffet. *Molletes*, fried eggs, sliced ham, and fruit. A tureen of *menudo* sat midway down the buffet, but Rachel passed it by, selecting only eggs and fruit with a couple of tortillas.

Rusty took ham, eggs, and potatoes and couldn't pass up the warm molletes with their melted cheese. He followed Rachel to the table and started to sit down, then remembered to pull out her chair. Immediately, a servant appeared and poured steaming coffee into their cups.

Domingo cleared his throat and addressed Rusty in

a booming voice. "I understand that your friend is recovering well."

Rusty set his cup back in its saucer. "Yes, sir, he is. Doc says he's developed no complications. We're waiting for his broken rib to heal up a bit more and we'll be out of your hair." He picked up his fork, then quickly added, "And we sure are grateful for your hospitality, while he mends."

Tía Maria chimed in. "I've had conversations with Señor Gentry while he's been here. I understand that he has his own horse ranch up north?"

"Yes, ma'am. He bought himself a few hundred acres in Missouri. He and his new wife are building a horse ranch there. That's why the stock he bought from Enrique Delgado is so important to him."

Rusty forked a bite of ham, but before it reached his mouth, Ana asked him another question. "Do you have a wife waiting in the north, as Señor Gentry does?"

Rusty's eyes widened. "No, I—"

"Ana!" Rachel snapped. She shot up straight in her chair and fixed her younger sister with a glare.

"Ana, that is not a polite question," Tía Maria said in a calmer tone.

Rusty held his fork mid-air, his eyes darting between the three females. He coughed and shoved the bite of food into his mouth.

Dr. Garcia appeared at the door of the dining room. "Good morning, everyone."

Rusty turned to see the smiling man walk into the

room. The air electrified as Tía Maria dropped her napkin to the table and half stood, then reconsidered and sat back down. She appeared to hold her breath as she watched him standing near the door.

"Doctor, please join us for some food." Domingo bellowed across the room.

Dr. Garcia dropped his medical bag and hat into a chair and strolled toward the dining table. "I've just examined my patient. He's doing well." Dr. Garcia seemed to be speaking to everyone, but his eyes were on Maria. He filled a plate and took the empty chair beside her.

Teresa, who had been quietly picking at her fruit, turned to her older sister. "Rachel, I suppose Paulo will be here this morning to escort you into Nogales for your dress fitting?"

Tía Maria shook her head. "No, no, no. The groom cannot take the bride-to-be for her fitting. He might see the dress." She looked at Rachel. "You will have to get one of the servants to drive you into town."

"There is no one who can do this on such short notice!" Domingo roared, his face taking on a deep red that matched the heavy velvet drapes. "Why did you not plan for this in advance?"

"I simply forgot about it." Rachel dropped her hands into her lap and turned to Rusty. "What are you doing today? Could you drive me to Nogales? It seems that I have forgotten a very important appointment with the dressmaker."

Tía Maria frowned at Rachel. "I have no objection to Señor Rusty driving you, but you must take Teresa or Ana along for the sake of propriety."

Teresa looked up sharply. "No, I can't do it. I have other obligations today."

Ana beamed. "I can go. I have no other plans."

Rusty gulped down a bite of food and looked around the table helplessly. "Well, yes ma'am. I reckon I could drive you." He took a swallow of hot, sweet coffee, wishing he could make a hasty exit from this table. Next time, he'd be sure to either eat with Jared or in the kitchen with the staff.

~

With Rusty's assistance, Rachel and Ana climbed into the carriage. He strode to the other side and hopped in beside Rachel. She smoothed the skirt of her yellow dress and opened her parasol. A current of excitement coursed through her. She felt eager — like she was on a special outing. She gazed across the miles of desert. Saguaro bloomed on either side of the road after the recent rain — red, pink, and white everywhere. They'd never been so stunning. Why did the desert look so beautiful today?

Rachel hadn't forgotten the dress appointment. She'd avoided it. Everything about her wedding plans depressed her. Her mood felt somehow lighter now. She glanced at the cowboy beside her with his hat pulled low over his hazel eyes. She smiled.

When they pulled up in front of Señora Cabrera's

storefront, Rusty secured the reins. "One moment, ladies, let me help you." He came around the carriage and took Ana's hand. She hopped to the ground and hurried to the boardwalk. Rusty turned to Rachel and put his hands on her waist, lifting her down as if she weighed nothing. The power in his hands sent a shiver up her spine.

Still close to her, he pushed his hat back. "How long do you think you'll be in there, Miss Rachel? I figured I'd head over to the general store and pick up a few supplies while I wait for you. Maybe send another telegraph to Jared's wife and let her know he's on the mend."

"Not more than an hour, I should think. Please, go ahead and take care of your business."

He tipped his hat to Rachel and started across the street.

~

His telegraph sent and purchases made, Rusty found an empty bench across from the dressmaker's shop and took a seat. He figured the ladies would take another half-hour visiting after they finished Rachel's fitting. He settled in and got comfortable. Leaning back, he pulled his hat lower and crossed his arms over his chest. A glint of light caught his eye, and he raised the brim of his Stetson. Across the street, Paulo Delgado strolled out of the bank, followed by two of his father's vaqueros. Paulo's silver concho hatband caught the sun and gleamed like a beacon.

Could Paulo be the man who'd sat on the ridge

watching the herd? It seemed far-fetched. Paulo was the son of a wealthy *hacendado* and he wanted for nothing. What reason would he have to be involved with horse rustling? Still, Rusty couldn't shake the thought.

The day after the incident occurred, Rusty had returned to the ridge overlooking Jared's herd. He'd searched the area for clues, but the rain had washed away any sign that might have been left behind.

Rusty watched as Paulo mounted his palomino and rode away, along with the two vaqueros. He wanted to tail them–to ask questions around town and find out who else in the area fit Paulo's description. He intended to make it his business to find out before he left for Missouri.

Chapter Five

Rachel stepped through the door of the dressmaker's shop and onto the boardwalk, Ana on her heels. Her smile dimmed. "Señor Rusty must be in one of the stores. I'm sure he'll be right back."

Before Rachel could decide her next move, she spotted Rusty striding across the street. "All done, ladies? I think we can make it back to the ranch before the sun gets much hotter."

"Certainly not." Rachel shook her head at this suggestion. "First we must go to the mission."

"The mission?" He glanced from one girl to the other.

"Yes, of course. Mission Tumacacori—or what is left of it." Rachel rested her hand on Rusty's arm and strolled back to the carriage. Ana stuck close to his other side. "Padre Antonio has made use of the abandoned mission to care for orphaned children. Bonita and Herberto have placed boxes of food and used clothing in the back of the carriage for us to deliver to the mission. We do this every month and today is our day to go again."

Ana agreed with Rachel. "And Cook has packed our lunch as well." She appeared to be inordinately pleased by this.

"Okay, and where is this mission?" Rusty first helped Rachel into the carriage and then Ana.

Rachel looked at Rusty as he settled in beside her. "Mission San José de Tumacácori is an old mission north of Nogales. It used to be our local mission, but the Apache attacked it so frequently that it was closed, and a new mission opened at Tucson—San Xavier del Bac. However, Padre Antonio still runs an orphanage there under the watchful eye of the *Federales*. Rachel lowered her voice conspiratorially. "It is also rumored they have bribed the Apache in some way to leave the mission alone. Not only that, but Father Antonio and his workers often have to drive off banditos. I've heard that Tubac is a hub for horse rustlers."

Rusty raised his eyebrows. "And your papá lets you ride out there once a month?"

"Oh, we're always accompanied by vaqueros." Rachel smiled up at him. "I trust you to keep us safe, Señor Rusty."

Rusty heaved a sigh. "Well. It looks like we're on our way to the mission to deliver supplies." He slapped the reins and turned the carriage north.

~

Half an hour into the ride, Rusty swiped a sleeve across his forehead. "Man, these desert summers are hotter than blazes."

Rachel reached behind the seat and retrieved a canteen. "Here. Have some water."

"Thank you, Miss Rachel." He took a drink and handed the canteen back to her.

"Rachel, I am so bored." Ana pulled at a thread on the sleeve of her blue dress and sighed. "I had forgotten how long this drive is."

"Stop your complaining, Ana. This monthly visit we make to the mission benefits others less fortunate than ourselves. It's a small sacrifice to make, even when it's not the most exciting drive."

Ana huffed and turned away.

Rusty reached under the carriage seat and withdrew a small paper bag filled with peppermint sticks. "I got these in the general store earlier. It might help a bit with the boredom." He passed the candy to Ana and Rachel, then took one for himself.

Ana's eyes went wide, and she popped it into her mouth with a grin. "Thank you, Señor Rusty."

"Miss Ana, this is a game me and my family used to play when we'd go on a long drive." He looked over at her. "I'll start. As high as…the stars in the sky. Now you, Miss Rachel. As high as…" Rusty trailed off.

Rachel turned to him and quirked an eyebrow. "Anything that is high?"

Rusty nodded.

"Alright then…as high as…an eagle's nest on a mesa." Rachel's eyes twinkled with enjoyment.

"Your turn, Miss Ana." Rusty grinned at her.

Ana rolled her big, dark eyes and then shrugged. "As high as Tía Maria's black mantilla."

Rachel giggled.

"Okay. As red as the evening sun on the horizon." Rusty looked to Rachel again.

She looked up for a moment. "As red as a bloom on a rose."

They both looked at Ana.

"As red as…Papá's face when you told him you forgot your dressmaker appointment this morning."

The sound of laughter rippled through the hot desert morning. The game became sillier and the laughter heartier as they drove toward the mission.

~

Gravel crunched under the wheels of the carriage when Rusty pulled up to the arched entry of the mission. Padre Antonio came running and helped Ana and Rachel down from the vehicle.

"Señoritas, how wonderful to see you! Please, come inside where it's cooler." Father Antonio looked to Rusty, who was unloading many boxes of supplies from the back of the carriage.

Rachel gestured toward Rusty. "This is Señor Rusty Cunningham. He and his friend are our guests for a while at the hacienda." Rusty came forward and shook hands with the priest.

"Please, everyone, come inside." Father Antonio waved them toward the entrance. "I'll ring the bell so the children will gather." He hurried inside and pulled the rope, causing the mission bell to clang.

From everywhere, children came running, almost knocking Rusty over as he carried in a box of supplies.

"Señorita Rachel!" The children gathered around, shouting her name, the littlest ones holding their arms out to her. She laughed and lifted a toddler and Ana hoisted a small child to her hip.

Rusty set down the last box, a broad smile creasing his face. "Padre, I'm hearing a lot of languages here, if I ain't mistaken."

"You are correct, sir. Here we care for orphaned and abandoned children of the Papago tribe, the Apache, the Pima, Yaqui, and, of course, Mexican children."

Rusty gazed at Rachel. "And they all seem real fond of Miss Rachel."

"Indeed, they are." Father Antonio smiled. "The Rios family are significant contributors to our mission. Not only with money, but much-needed supplies." He gestured toward Rachel. "As you can see, the children love her greatly. She never fails to bring special things for the children—not only new dresses for the little girls, but toys for all the children. She takes time to play and sing with them. Here at the mission, she's seen as an angel."

"I sure can see that," Rusty whispered. He lowered his head and peered at her from under the brim of his hat. It surprised and disconcerted him a little that when he looked at her, his pulse quickened.

Rachel put the children down and strode over to the

two men. "Padre, is that a new rope and timber for the bell tower?" She pointed to the items sitting in the corner.

"Yes, Señorita. They were delivered to us from Tucson two weeks ago, but to be perfectly honest, I have neither the strength nor the courage to climb up into the tower and make this repair." Father Antonio shrugged his shoulders. "Perhaps we can persuade a couple of men in Nogales to do this task for us."

Before he could think about it, Rusty spoke up. "I can do it for you, Padre. I'm afraid I don't have time today but I could come back in two or three days and make the repair for you."

Father Antonio beamed. "I would be most grateful, sir. Most grateful."

"Forgive us, but we don't have time to stay and visit with the children today." Rachel took Father Antonio's hand. "We had an appointment in Nogales before we came here that took up all our extra time."

"I understand, Señorita. I hope you'll be able to stay longer the next time you come to the mission."

"Yes, we'll be sure to come earlier next time." Rachel turned to Ana. "We'll go to the chapel now for prayer before we leave for home."

~

After discussing the repair to the bell tower and saying his goodbyes to Father Antonio, Rusty made his way to the chapel. He removed his hat and entered the cool, dim adobe building. At the end of the aisle, candles glimmered on the altar and the scent of incense filled the air. Rachel and Ana knelt, their heads veiled and bowed.

Rusty stood at the back of the church for a moment and took in the serenity of his surroundings. He lowered his head. *Lord, I've got a lot to thank You for, starting with sparing my friend Jared's life. It's only by Your mercy that the bullet didn't kill him.*

He lifted his head and looked at Rachel as she prayed. Maybe someday he'd have a girl like that. One that put serving God and helping others above herself.

He studied her. Beautiful inside and out. But she was about to marry another man and way above his station in life, anyway. Besides, he had plans of his own. He figured that within a couple of years, he'd have enough money saved to buy a ranch, much like Jared's. It was his vision for his future, and nothing would prevent him from achieving his dream.

A girl like Rachel was way out of his league, not to mention the difference in their culture. Rusty shook off those thoughts.

After his prayer, he quietly stepped out of the chapel into the dry Sonoran heat. He found a spot of shade to wait for Rachel and Ana so they could head home. Soon, the sisters exited the adobe and hurried toward him.

"One moment, Rachel. My throat is so dry." Ana ran to the well to draw water.

Rusty put his hands on Rachel's waist to lift her into the buggy, and she placed a hand on each of his forearms. She looked up into his face and murmured,

"Señor Rusty, I want to thank you for your kind offer to replace the crossbeam in the bell tower for Padre Antonio. Your help is so very appreciated." She stood on her tiptoes and feathered a kiss on each of his cheeks.

Fire seared through him, starting with his face, traveling down the length of his body, and shooting out his toes. He was lightning-struck. How was it possible? How could two small, baby-soft kisses turn a man inside out and upside down? He gazed into her dark, luminous eyes. He cleared his throat. "You're…you're welcome, Miss Rachel." He stammered and lifted her into the carriage.

He went to the other side of the buggy and stood for a moment, holding onto the arm of the seat. *Oh, help me, Lord. I'm a goner. I've got to get out of Sonora while I still have my head on straight.*

~

Rusty wandered into Jared's room, still dazed. He looked over to see Jared by the deep-set window writing a letter.

His friend glanced at him. "Hey, buddy. When you go to town next, would you post this for me?"

Rusty didn't respond but dropped into a chair and sat stone-still, staring straight ahead.

Jared looked at him again. "Rusty?" Jared put down his pen and turned in his chair to face him. He winced with the movement.

Rusty sat motionless, feeling the intensity of Jared's stare.

"You doing okay?" Jared squinted at Rusty.

"Yeah. I'm okay."

Jared gave a humorless chuckle. "Well, you look like you've had the devil scared out of you. Where have you been? Didn't you take Miss Rios and her sister to town for some dress fitting?"

"Yeah. I took her for a dress fitting. Then we went to the mission near Tubac to deliver supplies to the orphans." Rusty turned and stared out the window. "Then she kissed me on the cheeks."

Jared laughed—soft at first, then louder and harder. He laid a hand on his ribs and held them, then wiped a tear from his eye. "She kissed you on the cheeks? Is that what's got you acting like a moonstruck calf? Are you in love now?"

"You think it's funny?" Rusty whipped around and shot him a hard look. "She's engaged, you know. And a rich girl."

Jared chuckled again, but his face softened. "Yeah, but the girl only kissed you on the cheek. Why make such a big deal of it?"

Rusty rubbed his hands over his face and sighed. He shook his head slowly. "No. It's not a big deal."

He looked up and met Jared's eyes. "You're getting better every day. Do you think if I was to saddle up and ride out of here, you'd be able to make it to Tucson and catch a stagecoach on to Kansas City?"

Jared's mouth dropped open. "Well… yeah. I guess I could." His eyes widened. "This is serious, isn't it?

You're falling for that girl."

Rusty jumped up and began pacing. "No, that's loco talk. Of course, I'm not falling for her. I'm just going stir-crazy. I need to get out of here."

Jared's voice lowered. "Okay, buddy. You do what you need to."

Rusty heaved a heavy sigh. "Nah…of course, I'm not leaving you here alone, Jared. I was just blowing off steam. And I made a promise to the Padre out at the mission that I'd do some work for him." He shook his head again. "As a matter of fact, I've got quite a bit of unfinished business here."

He strode to the window facing the desert and set his gaze on a distant butte, with its hues of purple, orange, and pink. The beauty of the scene stirred him. A few pillowy clouds cast long shadows over the tabletop mesa north of the rancho. The ever-present scent of creosote and sage wafted through the window. A vision of Rachel and her little sister, laughing and playing their silly game as they traveled to the mission flashed into his mind. And the touch of Rachel's soft lips on his cheeks— no, he wouldn't allow himself to think of that. Instead, he turned back to Jared. "I'll bet the herd's getting close to Sedalia by now."

Jared nodded. "Yeah. They're never far from my mind. My future depends on that herd."

Rusty's thoughts turned to Paulo Delgado, the man he suspected of horse rustling and getting Jared shot. He hated the thought that Rachel might marry such a man.

~

As Rusty strode across the wide foyer toward the door, Domingo Rios called to him from his office.

"Cunningham, come in here for a moment, *por favor*." Rusty walked into the sunny room that smelled of tobacco and aged brandy. Seated at his massive mahogany desk, Señor Rios lit a cigar.

"What can I do for you, sir?"

"Please, sit down." He pointed to the heavy, carved chair in front of his desk.

Rusty took his seat and sized up the man before him. Short but powerfully built, with broad shoulders, he had a neatly trimmed goatee and a head of thick, wavy, graying hair. He motioned to the box of cigars on his desk, but Rusty shook his head, declining the offer.

Domingo leaned back in his chair and looked Rusty in the eye. "You and your friend, Mr. Gentry, have been here for a couple of weeks now?"

"Yes, sir, we have. Jared's getting better by the day and Doc says he'll be able to travel in about a week. But we can clear out of here right away if you want us to."

Domingo waved away the suggestion. "No, no, of course not. You're both welcome to stay until Mr. Gentry has recovered enough to travel." He blew out a puff of fragrant smoke. "You know, in many ways, you remind me of my father who came here from Spain. He left his family far behind and struck out on his own. He built this rancho with his bare hands. I see much of him in your personality and your desire to build your own ranch." He leaned forward on the desk. "I think you must be getting rather…bored with nothing much to fill your days while you wait."

Rusty grinned and raised his eyebrows. "Well, you're not wrong about that, sir. I've found a few things to do, but I am getting a bit restless."

Domingo nodded. "Well, I've been thinking. If you'd like to get out of the hacienda and feel useful, my vaqueros will be moving a large herd of horses to a new range with fresh water in a couple of days. If you'd like to go on this drive, it would be helpful to my men and would give you something to do."

Rusty agreed. "Sure, Señor Rios. I'd be glad to go. It'd be a way for me to earn my keep while I'm here."

Domingo smiled broadly. "Alright, it's settled." Then his eyes twinkled. "Oh, and tonight we're having a small dinner party. Paulo Delgado, Dr. Garcia, and Carlos Rodriguez, the son of one of our neighboring hacendados. You must attend." His tone was matter-of-fact.

Rusty raised his hands and shook his head. "Thank you, sir, but I'll pass on the dinner party."

"No, no, no, Cunningham. I insist that you attend. It will be nothing formal—just a small dinner. And if Mr. Gentry is up to it, we'd like him to attend as well." He stood up and swaggered around his desk as if the matter were decided. "We'll see you both downstairs at seven o'clock."

Chapter Six

The room glowed with soft candlelight when Rusty made his way into the formal dining room. If he had felt out of his element at the Rios breakfast table, he was in for an even greater awakening at dinner. The fifteen-foot table, laden with gleaming silver, crystal, and imported china, was a sight to behold. Four silver candelabras blazed with beeswax candles down the length of the table. Thick carpets covered the floor, magenta, emerald, and charcoal gray. *Man, won't this be a story for the boys back at the bunkhouse?*

When Rusty and Jared entered the room, they stood for a moment, taking in the ambiance. Domingo approached them. "Gentlemen." He turned to Jared. "I'm happy you were able to join us. I see that you are recovering nicely."

"Yes, thank you, Señor Rios. I'm most grateful for your hospitality these past couple of weeks. Your family has been so kind and gracious." Jared was still pale, but he'd talked all day about how eager he was to leave his sick room.

"It has been our great pleasure." Domingo gestured into the room. "Come with me. I'd like to introduce you to our other guests. Of course, you know Dr. Garcia." The graying physician bowed to Rusty as he took a *tapas* from a servant.

They crossed the room, and Domingo called out to two men huddled in the corner. "My neighbors Paulo Delgado and Carlos Rodriguez, please greet our American guests, Rusty Cunningham and Jared Gentry."

Paulo and Carlos both made slight bows to Jared. "*Mucho gusto.*" Carlos extended his hand to Jared, then Rusty.

Rusty's eyes latched onto Paulo's. "We've met a few times."

There was a sudden hush, and all eyes went to the entrance to the dining room. Maria Rios glided into the room, followed by Rachel, Teresa, and Ana. Rusty's eyes widened, and his stomach flip-flopped. Was this what they meant by the term lovesick? He sure felt like he wouldn't be able to eat a bite of food. No, he was not in love. The idea was crazy. There could never be anything like love between him and Rachel.

The four Rios women entered the room like royalty. Señora Maria's bearing was stately and regal, her back ramrod straight. Rachel followed Maria, then Teresa, and lastly, Ana. Rachel wore her black mantilla and an emerald-green satin dress. Around her neck, she wore a string of pearls with a cameo. Rusty couldn't take his eyes off her.

Paulo snapped a sharp look at Rusty. He slammed his glass on a nearby table and strode to Rachel. Placing one hand on her back, he took possession of her. Rusty clenched his fists. He despised Paulo's arrogance. How could Rachel ever be happy with such a man? He turned his back to them and walked away.

At dinner, Señor Rios held court from the head of the table. As the servants came around with roast chicken and vegetables, he addressed Jared. "Mister Gentry, I am not sure whether anyone has told you. Two vaqueros who are believed responsible for your shooting have been arrested." His voice boomed. "I hope this brings you some sense of justice."

Rusty's eyes went to Paulo. More and more, he suspected him of being involved behind the scenes with the horse rustling because the vaqueros were his father's men. Paulo glared at him from across the table.

"Yes, I'm certainly happy to hear that." Jared laid his hand on his chest over the area of his wound. "I'm glad to see this finally put to rest."

Jared turned to Paulo. "Señor Delgado, please convey my appreciation to your father. He kept his word to me and brought this to a swift conclusion. Hopefully, the men arrested are the ones truly responsible." Paulo nodded to Jared, his face tight and unreadable.

Rachel raised her glass to Rusty. "And let us not forget our friend, Mister Cunningham. He helped with the delivery to the mission today and has promised

Padre Antonio he'd repair the bell tower for him. The Padre was so grateful."

Murmurs of praise came from Señor Rios and Maria. "How wonderful," Maria said. Rusty gave a tight smile but wouldn't look at Rachel. Paulo's eyes shot daggers at Rusty.

With the main course finished, a servant brought caramel-topped flan and coffee around the table. Domingo addressed Jared. "I understand that you have a few hundred acres in Missouri that you will graze your newly acquired horses on."

Jared sat up straighter in his chair. "Yes, that's right. The new horses and a small herd of quarter horses I already own." He took a sip of his coffee. "I expect to have the best herd in western Missouri when I get home."

"And I think Mister Cunningham will be your neighbor with a ranch of his own, much as the Rodriguez family neighbors us?" Domingo took a sip of port.

"That will happen when the time is right." Rusty smiled over his cup of coffee. "Right now, I'm intent on helping Mr. Gentry get his ranch up and running. Then I'll worry about my own."

He glanced at Jared in the chair beside him. He could see he was near exhaustion from the effort of this evening. He leaned over and whispered to Jared. "Man, you look like the devil. You'd better call it a night and head upstairs before you fall out of your chair."

Jared nodded. "I think you're right."

He stood and looked first at Señor Rios, then

glanced around the table. "I hope you'll all excuse me. I've enjoyed this evening, but I think I've overdone it a bit. I'm going to head up to my room now."

From around the table, voices bid him goodnight. Domingo stood. "Of course, you must get your rest."

Rusty slid back from the table and grasped Jared's arm to stabilize him. "I'll help Jared upstairs and get him settled in."

"Yes, then please join us back here for after-dinner conversation. We still have some things to discuss." Señor Rios left Rusty with no choice.

~

Rusty jogged down the wide staircase and reached the huge, shadowy foyer. Only one lamp and a couple of wall sconces flickered in the dimly-lit room. At the foot of the stairs, Rusty came to a sudden stop. Rachel stood in one darkened corner. She hurried to meet him at the bottom stair.

Rusty, taken by surprise, tensed up. All evening, he'd done everything he could to avoid this moment of closeness with Rachel—a nearness he didn't want to inflict upon himself. He wanted to put a quick stop to the flicker of attraction he had for her.

He took a step in the direction of the great room where everyone gathered, but Rachel stopped him in his tracks. She put a hand lightly on his arm. "No, Señor Rusty."

He looked down at her. Even in the dim light, he could see the distress on her face. It was difficult for him to watch.

"Rusty, what have I done to offend you?" Confusion shone in her eyes. Her hand still touched his arm, and she slowly pulled it away. "I thought we were friends. I thought you and Ana and I enjoyed our day together. But all evening you've ignored me. You won't even speak to me. I don't understand what's happened. Why are you angry with me?"

Rusty wanted to pull her close, wrap her in his arms, and tell her he wasn't angry with her—quite the opposite. Instead, he backed away from her. "No, Miss Rachel, nothing is wrong. I'm not angry. I've just got a lot on my mind right now." He couldn't tell her she was making a horrible mistake by marrying Paulo. That, she deserved a man who'd cherish her till the day he died.

He backed up a few steps more. "I need to go speak to your father about the drive he wants me to help with. Excuse me."

He turned and almost ran from her. Rusty had to get away before he said or did something they'd both regret. He couldn't look at her again and see the hurt on her face.

In the great room, he stood to one side, waiting for his roiling emotions to settle. What did Señor Rios want to discuss? Maybe the horse drive to the new range. Rusty started toward the double doors leading to the patio for some fresh air.

As he neared the doors, he passed Paulo and Carlos Rodriguez huddled near the corner.

"Yes, Señor Rios is driving a sizeable herd to the

new range east of here the day after tomorrow. From what I've heard among the vaqueros, it will be some of the young mustangs he recently acquired. It will be a valuable herd." Paulo lifted his goblet and took a sip of garnet-colored liquid.

Carlos raised his eyebrows. "Is that so? You say they are driving them to a new range east of the rancho—the morning after tomorrow?" He scratched his cheek. "How many? So many beautiful horses added to his already enormous herd. And someday they will all be yours. How lucky a man is to be first-born in a family. The youngest son has no such advantage." Carlos looked at Paulo. "I suppose there will only be a few vaqueros driving them. I can't imagine that very many would be required…"

Paulo looked over and saw Rusty watching them. Carlos seemed startled and began to adjust his charro tie. He flinched and turned. "Really, you should have made your presence known."

"Should I? Well, now, I'm real sorry about that." A slow smile crept across Rusty's face. "I was just on my way outside for a bit of fresh air." He nodded to the men and walked away.

Oh, I'll be watching you two on the drive. You can count on that.

Chapter Seven

Rusty cracked open a sleepy eye. He lay still for a moment, allowing consciousness to seep through him. Taking the first quiet minutes of the morning to think over his plans for the day had been a habit since childhood.

He heard Jared stir in his bed, then struggle to sit up. Rusty got to his feet and helped Jared raise himself to an upright position.

Jared ran a hand through his untamed dark hair. "You know you don't have to sleep on the floor and babysit me. I'm getting better now."

"Yeah, you're getting better, but you still need some help to sit up with that sore rib."

Jared stretched and heaved a sigh. "I don't think I can take another day of sitting in this room. I need to get outside and do… something. These walls are starting to feel like a jail cell."

Rusty nodded. "Yeah, I reckon you are ready to get out into the sunshine for a while." He pulled on his boots. "How would you like to go for a little buggy ride? That should be easy enough on your ribs. I could show you around the ranch and we could have a talk."

Jared eagerly agreed. He reached for his shirt and pulled it on. "Let's get a bite to eat and get out of here for a while."

~

Red dirt coated the sides of the buggy as Rusty drove out onto the road leaving the hacienda. In the distance, a vineyard stretched across the horizon. Rusty gestured with one hand. "Look at that, Jared. Can you believe Señor Rios is growing grapes right here on the same enormous property where he's raising all these horses and cattle?" Rusty drove the horse at a slow, leisurely trot, avoiding ruts and bumps on the hard-packed road.

Jared squinted against the bright sun after almost two weeks behind closed doors. "Yeah, I hear some first-rate wine comes out of this valley."

They rode in silence, taking in the scenery. Jared's brows knit together as he looked at Rusty. "Okay, let me see if I have this straight. Paulo Delgado is the son of Enrique Delgado. We know it was a couple of Enrique's vaqueros that tried to get away with my stallions. And one of these two vaqueros shot me." He held himself carefully, half-turning to Rusty as he spoke. "Now you have a theory that Paulo is involved with the rustling that's been going on in the valley. And you think this because you saw someone sitting on the ridge above my herd, watching while you talked with Dave Fletcher? Do

I have this right?"

"Yeah, that and the silver hatband he wears. The man watching the herd had something silver that caught the sunlight. And I know Paulo rides a palomino."

"You might be right. I trust you and your instincts." Jared narrowed his eyes. "I don't suppose any of this suspicion might have anything to do with the fact that a certain Miss Rios seems to have—well, a bit of a crush on you? She's been paying you an awful lot of attention. And right offhand, I'd say you seem to be returning those feelings. Could that have anything to do with your dislike of the man?" He gave his friend a skeptical smile.

Rusty whipped his head around and bellowed at Jared. "How can you say a thing like that to me? I ain't returning any kind of feelings for Miss Rachel! Anybody can see she's a beautiful and sweet-natured girl. Way too good for that slicked-down dandy Paulo Delgado. I just don't want to see a girl like her end up married to a man like him. That's all." Rusty bunched his shoulders and then shook them loose. He sucked in a deep breath and blew it out slowly, trying to calm himself down.

"Okay…okay." Jared chuckled. "I just wanted to be sure you've really thought this through."

Rusty dipped his head. "Durned right, I've thought it through. And besides all that, I heard a piece of conversation between him and Carlos Rodriguez after supper last night. They were talking about the drive tomorrow morning. The one Señor Rios asked me to help with. Paulo seemed mighty interested in the herd and where we're gonna be driving the horses to."

Jared tilted his head. "Hmm. Is that so? Well, then maybe it's a good thing you're going along on this drive. But be careful, Rusty. We already know these men are willing to kill without giving it a second thought. I don't want you to end up shot like me."

"I'll be careful." A smile tugged at one corner of his mouth. "I only plan to do some nosing around when we're on the trail tomorrow. See what I can find out.'"

"In fact, we're kinda heading that general direction right now. I'd like to scout the terrain a bit before I'm responsible for driving over a hundred horses to new pasture." Rusty scanned the trail, his eyes following a hawk to a mesa in the near distance. The morning sun reflected shades of burgundy off the flat sandstone.

Rusty sucked in a deep breath of air and surveyed the countryside. "Look at this place, Jared. There's something special about it. Them reddish mesas off in the distance and the way the air smells. It's wide open and too wild for men to tame."

"Yeah, it's beautiful country, alright. But my heart's tied to a girl and a little ranch back in Missouri." He smiled but his eyes were sad. "I hope she still remembers who I am by the time I get back there."

Rusty's focused gaze took in the horizon. "Oh, I daresay she'll still remember you. Just you wait. A few more days and we'll leave this place behind." Rusty smiled, but Rachel's face flashed through his mind, and his heart clenched as he said the words.

He froze. "Jared, look! Did you see that?" He jutted his chin toward the mesa.

Jared aimed his gaze at the flat-topped ridge. "What is it? Yeah, I see that hawk."

"No, look again, but don't make any sudden moves." Rusty turned his head slowly. "I'll be danged if there ain't a rider up there watching us."

Jared eased his hat back, looked again, and shook his head. "Now, if this isn't a coincidence to end them all." He slid his hat over his brow again. "I see him, alright. There's somebody out there really interested in us."

Rusty drove on for a mile and found a wide place to turn the buggy around. "I suppose we've had enough sightseeing for this morning."

~

Rusty trotted Trueno, his borrowed horse, from the barn and turned toward the gravel drive. His thoughts fixated on the man he and Jared had seen that morning. Rusty intended to find out who he was and what he was up to.

At Cook's excited shouting, he halted and looked toward the back of the hacienda. At the kitchen door, Rachel stood at the tailgate of a wagon, lifting the covers from crates filled with food.

"Rosa, I can drive the wagon. It isn't the end of the world. Why should this food wait for Herberto to take it?" She re-covered one of the boxes and strode to the front of the cart.

"No, señorita. No! Your papá will be furious if he finds you drove a wagon of food to the workers in the vineyard."

Rachel gave an impatient sigh. "Let me worry about that, Rosa."

Cook threw her hands in the air and walked back into the kitchen, ranting something Rusty couldn't understand.

"Is there anything I can help you with, Miss Rachel?" Rusty looked down at her from the back of his horse.

"No, I can…well, maybe there is, if you don't mind." She smiled up at him from under her flat-crowned hat.

"I don't mind a bit."

"Perhaps you could help me take this food to the vineyard—"

"Okay, let me stable my horse and I'll drive it out there for you. We can't have your papá upset with you."

A moment later, he climbed into the driver's seat, to find Rachel sitting there holding the reins. She gave him a wide-eyed look. "I'll go with you. You won't know what to do once you get to the vineyard." She handed him the reins. "Here. You drive, please."

Rusty shook his head but said nothing. It would do no good to argue with this strong-willed girl. He slapped the reins and the wagon jolted into the driveway.

He pushed back his Stetson and gave Rachel a sideways glance. "Does someone take a wagon load of food to the vineyard workers every day?

"Oh, no." She raised her eyebrows. "But of course, you don't know. Tonight is the start of our grape harvest. We always harvest at night. This keeps the temperature consistent for the clusters and is easier on the harvesters. We make sure the workers have plenty of food and everything they need to make their task easier. It's an event everyone looks forward to." She continued. "I hope you and Señor Gentry will be here when the reaping is complete. The harvest celebration is a wonderful night of revelry."

Hoofbeats pounded up behind them. Rusty turned to see who was approaching at such a speed.

"Ana!" Rachel yelled in disbelief.

Ana galloped up beside the wagon, her hair flying behind her like a raven's wing. She tossed her head and laughed. "Rachel, I want to help, too. You thought you were going to leave me at home doing needlepoint, didn't you?"

"Ana, you are the most stubborn, headstrong, disobedient girl I know," Rachel shouted at her and crossed her arms tight over her chest.

Rusty mumbled. "Yeah. I can't imagine where she gets it from."

As they approached the vineyard he'd seen from a distance that morning, Rusty's eyes widened. Row after row, acre after terraced acre of vines, lay heavy with clusters of deep purple grapes.

Rachel directed Rusty to a wall tent where a

vineyard worker began unloading the wagon. Rusty jumped down and strode around the wagon, helping Rachel to the ground. Ana started to dismount but Rachel pointed a finger at her younger sister.

"Oh, no you don't. You're going straight back to the hacienda."

"I'll go when you do, Rachel." Ana smiled sweetly and slid down from her horse.

After they'd emptied the wagon, Rachel gazed up at Rusty. "Have you never been in a vineyard before? It's a beautiful place, especially when the grapes are ripe for harvest, as they are now."

He gazed at the neat acres of vines stretched out with perfect symmetry. "No, I sure haven't. I've never seen anything like it."

"Come. Let me give you a quick tour." She took his arm. "We'll borrow a couple of horses." Rachel led him down the long row of vines to a line of wagons. "The harvesters will pick the clusters and carry their baskets to these wagons where they'll deposit them. Then the grapes will go to the big presses to be crushed and filtered. After that, the juice goes into barrels for fermentation."

Rusty laughed. "It sounds a little more complicated than the white lightning they make back home."

She gazed across the gently terraced field. "Oh, it can get very complicated, indeed. One must get the correct blend of grapes—then there's fermenting, clarifying, bottling and aging. It takes generations of knowledge. Papá knows a lot about it, but he has a couple of wine masters working for him. He wants to perfect his wine and brandy."

Rusty let out a low whistle. "Your papá is an amazing man. He seems to be the best at everything he does." He smiled. "Everything from breeding horses to growing grapes and raising the most beautiful daughters in Sonora." He lifted the corner of his mouth. "Or any other place I've ever been."

Rachel blushed deeply. "Señor Rusty, what a very kind thing to say."

"Oh, I ain't being kind and I don't give idle flattery. If I say something, you can believe I mean it." He swept his gaze across her face, causing her to look away and blush again.

She cleared her throat. "We should get back to the tents. This tour took longer than I'd realized. The sun is already getting low in the sky." She nudged her horse and led the way up the row of vines to the front of the vineyard.

Halfway up the long path, they spotted Ana trotting toward them.

"There you are." Ana pulled up next to Rachel. "Come on…the harvesters are gathering and soon the musicians will be here."

"Musicians?" Rusty's mouth dropped open.

Rachel giggled and glanced back at him. "Yes, musicians. Papá does nothing in a small way. He believes music makes the harvesters work more efficiently."

Rusty shrugged. "Well, who am I to argue?"

At the front of the vineyard, the harvesters began arriving and musicians set up their instruments under a canopy. Workers unloaded barrels of water from a wagon while others prepared tables of food. Amazement filled him. This spectacle reminded him of the engagement fiesta he'd ridden in on the night Jared was shot.

Rachel busied herself helping with the preparations, never idle for a moment. He suddenly snapped back to reality. She was engaged and would soon be the wife of Paulo Delgado, a man he suspected of being a criminal. Rusty moved close beside her. "I'd best get you back to the hacienda, Miss Rachel. We've been here longer than I realized, and you'll have to go back with me in the wagon."

Rachel pivoted to him. "But there's no hurry. I want you to see some of the harvesting and enjoy the food and music. You may never get another chance."

"Well, ma'am, I can't argue with you about that. But your papá and Señora Maria are gonna be plenty worried and angry. I feel responsible for you since I drove you out here. I think I should get you and Miss Ana back to the house." He swept an arm toward the wagon.

Ana tilted her face to Rachel and arched an eyebrow. "My sister, I know how much you want Señor Rusty to enjoy this evening. Perhaps we can send one of the kitchen workers back to tell Papá where we are so he won't worry."

Rachel's face brightened. "Ana, sometimes you surprise me. That's an excellent idea."

From the front of the tents, a foreman stood in the back of a wagon and shouted. "Everyone—your attention, please. The harvest has begun!"

Musicians started to play a lively tune and the harvesters took their places at the head of the rows of grapes, cutting the ripe, purple clusters and depositing them into their baskets which they dragged beside them as they made their way down the path.

Rachel took Rusty by the arm and led him to one of the tents, reaching for glasses of cold lemonade for him, Ana and herself. The setting sun rested on the distant hills. Flaming streaks of magenta, pink and orange washed the horizon. A gentle breeze swept across the fertile field carrying the earthy scent of sweet, ripe grapes. Rusty gazed at the scene around him. *It almost seems like the good Lord just put His seal of approval on the harvest.*

~

"Rachel…Ana!" A familiar, angry voice rang out from beside them. "Your papá has been looking for you both."

There were Paulo and Teresa sitting their horses at the entry to the vineyard. She let out a deep sigh. "Paulo, how nice of you to come looking for us."

Paulo and Teresa dismounted and strode over to her.

"Papá intended to come and commence the harvest himself, but he has a pressing matter to deal with at home." Teresa reached for a glass of lemonade.

Rachel curled the corner of her mouth in a skeptical smirk. "And he sent the two of you to order Ana and me home?"

"He wanted Paulo to oversee the beginning of the harvest." Teresa moved close to Paulo's side.

"Yes. He knows that someday I'll be responsible for all this." Paulo spread his arms across the vista before them. "He wants to familiarize me with the operation."

Rachel couldn't help but roll her eyes.

"I think you and Ana should be on your way home." Teresa took a sip of her lemonade and raised her eyebrows imperiously.

"We're not ready to go home, Teresa. Rachel and I are showing our guest how Papá harvests his grapes. He'll be going back to his Missouri soon." Ana set her glass on a table. "If Papá was here, he'd let me help harvest this row of grapes." She sprinted down one of the long footpaths.

"Ana, come back here right now!" Rachel started to chase her but Paulo took her wrist.

"Let her go. She's having fun and we'll collect her soon to take her home." Paulo led them to a table covered with a cloth and baskets of bread, wine, fruits and cheese.

The four of them sat down and took in the

bustling scene. Teresa gazed up at Paulo and rested her chin on her fist. "Yes, someday you'll make a wonderful hacendado. You'll be in charge of everything you see here and much, much more."

Paulo's eyes became thoughtful. "Teresa, it isn't that I desire to be in charge of a vast rancho and all the possessions and wealth that come with it." Paulo's eyes were thoughtful. "This is what I was born to do. Our grandfathers came to this country with nothing but their wits and strong hands to build these vast empires for us." He visually swept the beauty around him. "It is my duty to tend what they created. My duty and my privilege."

For a moment, Rachel admired Paulo. She had a glimpse of a side of him she'd never seen before. She moved her eyes to Teresa who sat next to him, gazing up at him, her eyes misted over, oblivious to anyone else in the vicinity. *She's in love with Paulo.*

"What an honor it would be." Teresa sighed. "What an honor for a woman to wake up every morning and oversee the tending of a great *casa*, her husband and children. To raise the next generation to carry on in our proud traditions." She nodded. "Yes, I understand your love for our customs."

A look passed between Paulo and Teresa. How perfectly matched they were and how poorly she and Paulo.

Rusty stood. "Excuse me, Miss Rachel. I'm gonna go take a little stroll. It's getting noisy in here. He strode to the path leading out of the vineyard and Rachel jumped up to follow.

Paulo held out a hand toward Rachel.

"Let her follow him," Teresa said. She touched Paulo's arm. "Let's sit here and enjoy the music and food." She smiled at him. "Soon enough, you'll have Rachel as your wife. But for tonight, just enjoy being a young *caballero* without a care in the world."

Outside the vineyard, Rusty leaned against the wheel of a wagon and gazed heavenward where stars were just beginning to blanket the night sky. Rachel swept up beside him.

"Señor Rusty, what do you think of our grape harvest?

Rusty shook his head slowly and chuckled. "Well, Miss Rachel, I'll say one thing for your family. You don't do anything in a small way, whether it's giving an engagement party, or harvesting grapes, or even eating breakfast." He gestured back at the vineyard. "This time spent with your family is something I'll always remember."

Rachel's smile faded. "You'll be leaving soon, no?"

He nodded. "Yes, I've got to get home. That's where my life is. It's nothing like what you're used to, that's for sure, but it's a good life. It's where I belong."

"I can see the beauty in this life you're returning to." She stood close to him and looked into his gentle eyes. "The important thing is to be with the one you truly love, whether it's on a horse ranch in Missouri or an estate in Sonora. If you have no peace in your soul, you'll not be happy anywhere."

The music slowed to a waltz. "The workers will rest now. They'll get their food and drink and relax for a while."

Rusty moved a strand of hair that had blown across her face. The music drifted to them on a breeze that carried the scents of the desert, mingled with the foods inside the vineyard.

"Miss Rachel, if any man on this earth has two left feet, it's me, but would you like to dance?"

She looked up at him and felt a smile tug at her mouth. "Yes, I would."

He took her hand in his large one and pulled her nearer. She placed her other hand on his shoulder. They began to sway gently with the music. She inched in closer and lifted her face to him. For a moment it brushed his neck and she caught the dizzying scent of his skin. He wrapped his hand tighter around hers and peered into her face, so close she could feel his breath on her cheek.

No, Paulo could never make me feel this way. Not if we lived together for a hundred years.

The music stopped and she and Rusty stood still, his lips near hers. "Miss Rachel. I…"

"Rachel, Rachel!" Ana came charging from the vineyard and skidded to a halt next to them. Her little sister looked up at her, a knowing smirk on her eleven-year-old face.

"Paulo is looking for you."

Rachel closed her eyes and exhaled. "Tell him I'll be right there."

~

Rachel woke up late the next morning. She would never have dreamed when she decided to drive a wagon of food to the vineyard that it would lead to her and her sisters staying late at the harvest commencement and having what amounted to a party.

Her brain was filled with nothing but Rusty Cunningham—his touch, his voice, the scent of him. She'd danced with him for just a short time but she could still feel his arms around her.

The sun's position was higher than usual and she turned on her side and gazed out the window. Yes, she'd slept in late and no doubt her sisters had, too. A tap on her door snapped her out of her reverie.

"Come in, Bonita." She recognized her maid's distinctive knock when she heard it.

Bonita entered the room with a tray laden with a cup and saucer, pot of tea and a breakfast roll. "It's time to get up, Señorita. It's getting late and you have things to do today."

Rachel sat up and stretched. "Bonita, give me a moment to open my eyes."

"Drink your tea. Your Tía Maria is already asking where you are." She opened the wardrobe and pulled out a dress for Rachel. "You'd better hurry. Both your papá and tía are very unhappy at you and your sisters after last night's behavior."

"I was sure they would be." Rachel slid out of the bed, lifted her cup to her lips and hurried behind the dressing screen. Perhaps she could stay busy with other things and avoid Papá and Tía Maria until much later.

~

Rachel knocked on Jared's bedroom door. At his reply, she opened the door and entered, Dr. Garcia following her into the room.

"Good morning, Señor Gentry. Dr. Garcia is here, maybe for your last visit if all goes well." She looked at the window with its drawn curtains. "No, you must open the curtains. It's a beautiful day and the sunlight will do you good." She slid back the drapes and the room flooded with light, turning the creamy walls a vibrant lemon yellow. "There. That's much better."

She flashed a smile at the two men. "I'll leave you alone now. I'll be back soon to see you out, Dr. Garcia."

A half-hour later, Rachel knocked at the door again.

Jared sat on the edge of his bed, his expression serious but hopeful as he waited for Dr. Garcia to speak. He slowly buttoned the last button on his shirt.

"Señorita." Dr. Garcia nodded to her as she came in the door. "I was just leaving. I believe Mister Gentry is well enough to travel home."

Rachel raised her eyebrows. "Oh? So soon?" She clasped her hands together. "Surely he hasn't recovered enough from his terrible injury to travel over a thousand miles?"

"Oh, he's a young and strong man." Dr. Garcia smiled. "He's healed very quickly."

The doctor folded his stethoscope and stuck it into his faded leather medical bag. "I think you've recovered well. I know your ribs are still tender and you haven't completely regained your strength, but I believe you can travel home next week if you feel up to it." He snapped his bag closed. "I won't give you any more of the pain medication. From today on, you'll need to depend on this tincture of willow bark." He handed Jared a new bottle containing a thick brownish liquid. "Use the laudanum only when you're in extreme pain while traveling or if discomfort is keeping you awake at night."

Dr. Garcia pulled his jacket on and tugged at the hem. "We, in the medical field, have recently come to realize that laudanum can become habit-forming, so it's up to you to ration your dosage. Use it only if absolutely necessary."

Jared's eyes widened. "You bet, Doc." He examined the bottle of willow bark tincture. "I never really liked the way that laudanum made me feel, anyway. Thank you, doctor. I sure do appreciate everything you've done for me." He extended his hand and Dr. Garcia shook it.

"You're most welcome, Señor. Safe travels back to your homeland."

Rachel stood silently. Her eyes went to the stack of quilts in the corner of the room where Rusty made his bed. "Well. I am certainly happy to hear this good news," she whispered.

Dr. Garcia tipped his hat to her and took his leave.

Rachel turned to Jared and forced a smile. "I hope you won't feel rushed to leave our home. We want you to recover completely before you attempt such a long journey."

"Thank you, Miss Rachel." Jared took hold of the bedpost and pulled himself upright. "You and your family have been so kind and hospitable, but I need to get home."

Rachel hung her head and nodded.

"I'll talk to Rusty about it, but I figure we'll hit the road early next week," Jared said.

Rachel fought to keep her composure. How could this be happening so soon? She didn't want Rusty to leave. *If he goes, I'll never see him again.*

"I understand." She grabbed a stack of clothes piled in a wicker basket. "I'll take these things downstairs to be laundered."

Rachel flew from the room with the laundry in her arms, racing down the stairs without watching where she stepped.

~

Rusty stepped inside the cool, thick adobe walls of the foyer. He'd just spent an hour training Diablo. He pulled off his leather work gloves, stuck them in his hat, and strode toward the staircase, his long legs eating the space quickly.

Suddenly, he heard a squeal, followed by a thud and the sound of someone falling. Rusty dropped his hat and raced the small distance to the staircase. A tumbling mass of black hair and pale clothing cascaded toward him. He flew up the last few stairs and caught the startled girl, stopping her fall.

Rachel looked up at Rusty, her eyes dazed and unfocused.

"Miss Rachel. What happened? Are you okay?" He picked her up and carried her into the great room. Rachel wrapped her arms around his neck and groaned.

He sat her down on a cushioned sofa and knelt beside her. "What in the world happened? Are you hurt?" He stroked her cheek and brushed back the silky hair that had come undone during her fall.

Rachel blinked and shook her head from side to side. "I think so. Oh, I feel so foolish! I've run down those stairs a thousand times—I can't imagine what happened today." She sat up and put her feet on the ground, then let out a gasp.

"What is it?" Rusty grabbed her hand.

"My ankle. I must have turned it as I fell down the stairs." She lifted her right foot and wrapped her hand around it.

"Lay back against the pillows for a minute. You shouldn't even try to walk. You might have broken it." Rusty lifted her leg, removed her slipper, and slowly rubbed her ankle and foot. "Does that hurt?"

She murmured. "No."

He rotated her ankle and wiggled her toes. "I don't see much swelling yet. I don't think you broke anything." Rusty gazed at her as she reclined on the gold-hued sofa cushions, her hair loose and her eyes wide and trusting. He gulped and set her foot gently on the floor.

"Put your arms around me, Miss Rachel. I'm taking you upstairs and going to find somebody to wrap that ankle." He leaned in close and lifted her arms around his neck.

A small sigh escaped her lips.

"What is it? Are you in pain?" He tried to look at her, but she held him fast.

"Señor Gentry said you're leaving in a few days. Nothing will be the same after you're gone." The anguish in her voice tugged at his heart.

"Miss Rachel…" Rusty turned his face to look at her and explain. Her face was so close he could feel her warm breath on his cheek. Then, as if of its own volition, his mouth was on hers, and he kissed her greedily…a kiss so urgent and sweet, it overpowered his senses. He pulled her close and held her against his chest. She wrapped her arms tighter and kissed him as though she'd never let him go.

Moments later, Rusty pulled away from her. He hung his head and rubbed his hands over his face. "I'm sorry."

"No, please don't say you're sorry."

"But I am sorry. I never meant for that to happen. I was out of line."

Rachel turned her head. "My mind and heart won't accept that you're leaving and I'll never see you again. Never hear your voice again." Her arms were still around his neck.

Rusty's mind raced. He knew he should get up and run from her, but he sat frozen in place. "Miss Rachel. You'll be married soon. Married to someone from your station in life. A rich man with noble blood." He stroked her hair. "Paulo and me—we're as different as night and day."

She bowed her head. "Yes, and you believe that is a problem. I see it as a breath of fresh air." She leaned back and touched his cheek. "You don't seem to understand how much I admire the man that you are."

Without a word, he picked Rachel up and headed back toward the staircase. As he walked through the arched doorway, Rusty stopped in his tracks.

Rachel's sister, Teresa, stood on the other side of the entry, her face stony and unreadable.

Chapter Eight

They strode past Teresa, pausing for only a moment. Rachel clung to him as Rusty carried her upstairs, opened her bedroom door, and slipped into the dimly lit, pastel-colored room. He made his way to the bed and laid her gently in the middle of a mound of feather pillows.

She still hadn't let him go. Rusty grasped her softly by the arms and pulled them away from his neck. He looked down into her eyes. "I'll get someone to wrap that ankle of yours, Miss Rachel." He turned and trudged out the door.

Rachel raised up on her elbows in bed and scooted higher on her pillows. She watched as Rusty strode out the door, and it clicked shut behind him. She leaned her head back and fought the tears that once again threatened to pour. Her ankle hurt, but that wasn't what caused her the real pain. She finally had to admit it to herself. The man she loved just walked out the door, and within a week, he'd walk out of her life forever if she didn't find a way to stop him.

And she intended to find a way to stop him. While most girls swooned over Paulo, she knew she didn't love him. In fact, he repelled her with his strutting arrogance and his idle, self-centered, aristocratic mindset.

Rusty Cunningham made her pulse race when he came near. His tall, strong build, his thick auburn hair, and hazel eyes. His deep voice and the slow way he spoke—it all affected her in a way she knew she'd never find again in any other man. And he had such a kind, gentle, and giving nature. She'd made up her mind. Rusty Cunningham was the man she wanted to spend her life with.

The bedroom door opened again, and Tía Maria entered with a roll of bandages. She stood at the door for a moment, looking at Rachel and not saying a word. Slowly, she made her way across the room and sat down on the edge of the bed.

"Rachel, my sweet girl." She lifted her niece's foot, examined her ankle, then laid it back on the bed. She patted her leg. The expression on her face and the tone of her voice worried Rachel.

"Is something wrong, Tía? You seem upset."

Maria sighed and began to unroll the long strip of cloth and wrap Rachel's ankle. She paused and looked into Rachel's face. "Mija, you cannot have this American cowboy." She looked down again and resumed wrapping the bandage. Her thick black hair shone in the lamplight, reflecting off the strands of silver at her temples.

Rachel stuttered. "What…what are you saying? I

am surprised you would speak to me this way." Rachel crossed her arms stubbornly.

Her aunt looked up again. The corners of her mouth tugged down as she gave Rachel a dour, knowing look. "My dear, don't you think I have seen the glances you have cast on this man —and the lovesick way he gazes at you when you are not watching?" She shook her head slowly. "No, it can never be. You must marry one of your own people, someone of your station in life." She took Rachel's hand and patted it tenderly. "Yes, Señor Rusty may be a very nice man, and you may find him attractive, but he'll return to his home far from us, and you will stay here and marry Paulo." She smiled, her eyes sad.

"Your Papá expects you to marry wisely. Marrying Paulo would keep the group of wealthy hacendados together—keep the land intact and the families strong. It's the way of our people. As the eldest daughter, it is your duty." She brushed Rachel's hair away from her cheek. "You will marry Paulo, produce three or four beautiful children who will grow up, and repeat the process. You and Paulo will buy more land, more horses, more cattle, grow more grapes and entertain lavishly. This is what the family expects of you, my sweet sobrina." Her eyes were solemn. "This is the way it must be." She leaned forward, wrapped her arms around Rachel, and hugged her.

Rachel closed her eyes, and tears streamed down her cheeks. Tía Maria stood and walked to the door. "You should rest here for the remainder of the day. I'll send Bonita up to you with a tray." She wrapped a hand around the doorknob and turned it.

"Tía Maria."

She turned back to her niece. "Yes, Rachel?"

"Did you love your husband?"

Tía Maria stood still as a statue for a moment, then answered stiffly. "I have never been married."

Rachel sat up straight. "What? How did I not know this about you, Tía? I've always assumed you were a widow since you returned from Spain. And you are called Señora."

Tía Maria looked across the room into the dim corner, not at Rachel. "Yes, it is a custom to call older ladies Señora, even when they have never married."

Rachel leaned against the pillows again. "I'm sorry, Tía. I didn't mean to pry. I just always thought someone as beautiful as you would have married."

Maria turned to Rachel, her eyes haunted. "I'll send Bonita to you, dear. Rest well." She slipped out the door.

~

Thunderheads building in the north threatened to cover the beauty of another Sonoran sunrise. A man never knew what the day would bring in the rainy season.

Rusty didn't relish the idea of spending half a day riding in the rain, but at least it would settle the dust the horses kicked up. He pulled a bandana over his nose and rode out to the side of the herd. A vaquero by the name of Alvarez rode point, and Carlos rode drag, where he dropped in and out of sight. Rusty and another vaquero rode flank to the sides of the herd as lookouts for any horses that might decide to stray.

They headed south, and by mid-morning, he wore his slicker and pulled his hat low to keep the rain out of his eyes. The rain felt mighty good and looked even prettier when they descended into a valley with the greenest grass Rusty had seen since coming to Sonora. By noon, they'd reached a good-sized body of water and were still on Rios land.

Rusty figured there were more than a hundred horses in this herd they drove into the verdant valley. It wouldn't have been hard for a few men to separate a couple of dozen horses from the group when they made the descent from the higher country into the basin, but Rusty knew they'd choose their time more carefully.

He had Paulo marked as being behind the rash of rustling going on in the area. He'd decided that the real reason Señor Rios had asked him to take part in this drive was to help his vaqueros protect the herd. Rusty intended to make it his business to prove that Paulo was behind this cattle rustling. He wanted to show Rachel's papá that Paulo was not the one for her. The thought of her being married to such a man tormented Rusty.

He'd watched and waited for Paulo this morning as they began the drive, but he didn't show up. Paulo wasn't here with his confidant, Carlos Rodriguez, as Rusty had expected. Perhaps he'd show up at their camp tonight. Or maybe one of these vaqueros acted as his agent in the rustling.

They began their descent into the basin. The magnificent sight of strong, wild horses running before him thrilled Rusty every time he saw it. He admired their raw power.

At sunset, after a supper of frijoles and jerky, Rusty leaned against his saddle, sipping a cup of coffee. The smell of creosote wood burning in the fire drifted on the breeze. Carlos Rodriguez stretched out on his blanket, rolled a cigarette, and smoked it. One of the vaqueros strummed a mandolin and sang some lonesome-sounding song. The drone of gentle music and singing soothed the horses just as it did cattle. It soothed the men, too, he reckoned.

Rusty's thoughts drifted to Rachel and the kiss they'd shared. Maybe it was possible. Maybe they could be together if she discovered Paulo to be a thief. Maybe Rusty could build up his own ranch quickly and be successful. No, that would take years of hard work and lots of money. He tossed and turned on his bedroll. *No, it could never happen. Me and Rachel can never be together.*

~

Chattering voices and laughter drew Rachel like a magnet. She hobbled down the staircase and entered the great room. Tía Maria, Dr. Garcia, and Ana were gathered around a table playing a card game, and from the sound of it, Ana was winning.

"Rachel, what are you doing down here? Dr. Garcia told you to stay in bed and keep that foot elevated." Tía

Maria placed her cards face down on the table.

"I'm sorry, tía, I couldn't sit in that room alone for another moment." She hopped closer and grabbed the back of a chair for balance. "It sounds like you're having fun in here."

Dr. Garcia jumped up and hurried to her side. "But Rachel, you need to stay off your sprained ankle." He took her arm and led her around to sit in the chair.

"Couldn't I play cards with you? I could put my foot up on another chair and keep it elevated."

Dr. Garcia shot a glance at Maria and shrugged. "I suppose it would be okay for a while." He helped Rachel to the card table and pulled up another chair for Rachel to rest her foot on.

"Now we can play Whist." Ana ran to get a cup of tea for her sister.

Rachel sighed with satisfaction and watched as Dr. Garcia reshuffled the deck of cards. "Where is Papá this evening?" Even as Rachel asked the question, she was happy she'd been able to avoid him all day.

Tía Maria took a sip of her tea. "He is out inspecting the grape harvest. He was so disappointed that he couldn't participate in the Commencement, but I'm told that it went very well."

Rachel beamed. "Oh, Tía, we had so much fun. It was a perfect evening. The weather wasn't too hot and the food was wonderful. You really should have come to the vineyard and joined in."

Maria picked up her cards and sniffed.

"Hmm…perhaps I should have. It seems that you three girls need someone older to keep a watchful eye on you every moment."

Rachel and Ana glanced at each other and then picked up their cards.

~

A sharp sound broke into Rusty's sleep. Barking. He raised up on one elbow and listened. Carlos was not in his bedroll. Alvarez's dog stood at the edge of camp and growled in the direction of the horses. Rusty snatched his rifle from its scabbard, crept to the *remuda*, and mounted his horse without a saddle.

He softly clicked to the gelding and rode toward the commotion. Images of the night of Jared's shooting flashed through his memory. The same scenario played out before him now. Voices whispered in the distance.

Rusty understood very little Spanish, but he heard one say to the other, *"Apresúrate, Benito,"* and two vaqueros walked their mounts through the restless horses. Rusty nudged his blue roan around the outside of the herd and crept up on the two thieves. He raised his rifle and levered a cartridge. The two men stopped dead still.

"Get out of there, or I'll shoot you down." Rusty had no idea if they understood him, but he figured they understood his tone of voice — low and deadly. They began to ride toward him. He couldn't see in the dim light if either of the men was Paulo Delgado or Carlos Rodriguez. "Drop your guns." They lowered their hands to their gun belts as if ready to drop them when the dog growled and charged.

Rusty's horse whinnied and reared. The two vaqueros took advantage of the moment, raced past him, and charged away into the tree line. Rusty raised his rifle, but they were already in the trees, and he couldn't afford to spook the animals. He lowered his gun. They were gone, and they'd taken horses with them. He felt sure one of these men had to be Carlos.

At sunrise the next morning, Rusty opened his eyes and sat up. Carlos lay across from him in his bedroll, sound asleep as if nothing had happened. Rusty rubbed his eyes and ran a hand through his shock of uncombed hair. He had to go today to do repairs at the mission, but he'd get to the bottom of this. He'd figure it out one way or another.

~

Rachel opened her eyes and blinked at the bright morning sun beaming through her bedroom window. She rolled onto her back and stretched. Her ankle was still stiff. Tía Maria had wrapped it, maybe a little too tightly. She sat up and put her feet on the cool tile floor, then stood and took a tentative step. Her ankle was sore, but she had a task to do today, and no inconvenient sprain would prevent her from accomplishing her mission. She sat down at her dressing table and pulled a brush through her hair. Thoughts of Rusty already filled her mind. In a few short days, he'd be leaving Sonora to begin the long journey to Missouri, leaving her forever.

There was a light tap on her bedroom door. She laid

down her hairbrush and turned from the mirror. It must be Bonita with her breakfast tray.

"Come in." The door handle turned, and Rachel said over her shoulder, "Bonita, please get my clothing ready for me. I have an errand to do this morning after I have my breakfast."

"And what errand will you be doing so early this morning with your sore ankle?"

Rachel's head snapped up at the sound of Teresa's voice.

"Oh. Good morning, Teresa. I thought you were Bonita with my breakfast tray."

Teresa crossed the room and took a seat in the creamy white, velvet-covered chair next to Rachel's dressing table. She sat stiffly, her back ramrod straight. Rachel could almost feel the anger radiating from her sister.

"What is it, Teresa?" Rachel sighed and steeled herself for the tongue-lashing she knew was coming.

Teresa raised her eyebrows and scooted to the edge of her chair, ready to do battle. "Tell me, my sister. Have you taken leave of your senses?" She raised her voice, and her face grew red with anger. She gestured wildly with her hands. "You are engaged to be married to the most handsome and…and wonderful man in Sonora, yet you continue to throw yourself at this… gringo American cowboy. What is wrong with you? You should be preparing for your wedding to a magnificent man."

Rachel stood and limped to the heavy mahogany

wardrobe. She took out a blue button-up blouse and her riding skirt. She pulled her boots from the back of the wardrobe.

Teresa rose from her seat so suddenly that she knocked it over. "You let that man kiss you, Rachel!"

"Yes, I did. And if I get my way, he'll kiss me again." She turned on Teresa and smiled. Teresa looked like she might have apoplexy.

"This is outrageous. He'll be gone in a few days, and you'll have to go back to behaving like a woman of your station. A woman about to marry the most desirable man in Mexico."

Rachel stepped behind a dressing screen, threw off her lacy white nightgown, and shrugged into the blue blouse. "Well, since you find Paulo to be the most handsome and desirable man in Mexico, why don't *you* marry him?" She slipped into the riding skirt.

Teresa strode to the window and then whirled around to Rachel, her face mottled with anger. "Oh, believe me, my sister. If I were the oldest daughter and engaged to Paulo, I'd be the happiest girl in Sonora. But you continue to upset him with your cold and indifferent behavior." She strode over to stand in front of Rachel.

Rachel pulled on her boots and stood. She looked Teresa in the eye. "I don't love Paulo. I would even go so far as to say that I don't really like him." She arched her eyebrows and raised her voice. "Take him for yourself, Teresa. You have my blessing."

Tears welled up in Teresa's eyes, and she spat her

angry words. "You know that isn't possible. *You're* betrothed to Paulo." She tossed her long black hair behind her shoulder. "But if you continue your inappropriate flirtation with Señor Cunningham, I'll report your behavior to Papá. This, I guarantee you." She whirled around and stomped to the bedroom door, which opened just as she reached it. A startled Bonita entered the room with Rachel's breakfast tray. Teresa stormed out the door, slamming it soundly behind her.

~

Rachel hobbled out the kitchen door and found Herberto waiting with her horse saddled and ready to go. "They have readied your horse. I have put your canteen here, and Rosa has packed a lunch for you in your saddlebag." He helped Rachel into the saddle. "Are you sure you want to go out alone today, Señorita? I'd be happy to accompany you. Your Papá would be beside himself if he knew you went into the desert alone."

"No, thank you, Herberto. I'm quite sure I'll be fine. Besides, I'm not really going that far."

At that moment, Ana flew out of the kitchen door and raced to Rachel's side. "I want to go with you. Take me. Can I go with you to the mission?"

Rachel shot an annoyed look at her little sister and shushed her. "No, you can't go this time, Ana. And who said I was going to the mission?"

"I heard you tell Bonita." She tugged at Rachel's boot. "Let me go with you," she pleaded. She peered up at Rachel from under her lacy eyelashes. She said a little too innocently, "You don't want Papá to know where you're going, do you?"

Chapter Nine

Rachel closed her eyes and held her head up as she prayed for patience. She'd told Bonita where she was going today because she wanted to visit the chapel for prayer, but more importantly, she wanted to speak to Padre Antonio for counsel on how to break her engagement with Paulo. She'd made up her mind she wouldn't marry him, no matter how angry her father became.

She spoke through clenched teeth. "Alright." She leaned down and whispered in Ana's ear. "But you must promise to keep my secret. Everyone must think I'm simply making a shopping visit to Nogales."

An enormous smile burst across Ana's face. "Yes, sister. I'll keep your secret."

Rachel looked back at the kitchen worker. "Herberto, please arrange for a buggy for us as quickly as possible." She turned to Ana. "And you, my little imp of a sister. Get a hat and two parasols."

Ana raced into the house to do as Rachel had instructed, then hurried back.

Rachel slapped the reins, and they rolled down the long drive toward the road. "Duck down. I don't want anyone to see you from the windows and know you're with me." Ana giggled and slid down to the floor of the buggy.

Once they were away from the house, Ana climbed back into the seat.

Rachel frowned at her. "I don't see why you wanted to come with me. The last time we made this trip, you complained that you were hot and bored."

Ana gazed up at her older sister. "I didn't want you to be alone." Her young face lined with worry then her lips curved into a sly smile. "And I know you're hoping to see Señor Rusty."

Rachel huffed and slapped the reins harder. "Ana, you really need to concern yourself with the things of an eleven-year-old girl and not those of your older sister." Still, she leaned over to Ana and kissed her cheek.

~

Rusty turned his tall roan toward the Mission near Tubac. He was riding out of the green valley and into the dry heat of the desert. After promising Padre Antonio to put up the new crossbeam for the mission bell, he meant to keep his word. And the promise to himself to prove Paulo was involved with the horse rustling going on in the valley. Rusty hoped to make that happen last night, but Paulo was nowhere around when the horses were stolen from Señor Rios's herd. However, he was certain now that Carlos Rodriguez had been a part of it.

Rusty's thoughts were all of Rachel — when she'd asked him not to leave, her pleading eyes, scent, and the warmth of her kisses. He shook his head vigorously. No, best not to think about that. Today, get the repair done for Father Antonio, then tomorrow or the next day, he and Jared would start for home. Rachel would marry Paulo or some other hand-picked caballero, and he'd forget about her when he got back to Missouri. But he knew it was a lie.

Just a few miles to the mission, a couple of hours to get the bell hung, and this day would be over.

Trueno took a faltering step and slowed his gait, lifting one leg carefully.

"Whoa, fella." He dismounted and lifted the horse's hoof, and checked for a rock or other debris that might be lodged in the crevices. "What's got you lame, buddy?" Rusty examined his ankle and leg for swelling or heat in the joint. He patted the stallion's shoulder.

"Well, I don't see what it is that's made you lame but I'd better get you home and let Pedro give you a good going-over." Just a short delay and then on to the mission.

~

Rusty swept into the bedroom like a tornado.

"What's got you in such a tizzy?" Jared stopped mid-motion as he threw his belongings into a saddlebag.

"I was on my way to the mission and my horse came up lame. I had to come back here for a fresh mount. This is gonna slow me up by at least an hour." He grabbed a clean shirt from his bag and stripped off his dirty one. "It's gonna be a long hot day working in that bell tower."

There was a knock at the door.

"Come in." Rusty straightened his collar and finger-combed his hair.

Maria Rios opened the door and glided across the room. It must have been a learned art. All cultured ladies seemed to know how to cross a room as if their feet never touched the floor.

"Ma'am." Rusty quickly tossed his packed saddlebags into the corner. "How are you this morning?"

She lifted her full lips into a wide smile revealing perfect, white teeth. He was struck, as always, at Señora Rios's loveliness. She must have been a devastating beauty in her youth.

"The question is, how are *you* this morning?" She glanced at Jared, then the stack of his belongings on the table near the bed. "Dr. Garcia tells me you're well enough to travel home, and it seems you're preparing to leave soon."

Jared nodded. "Yes, if Rusty gets a few things wrapped up today, we'll be heading home in the next couple of days." He took a small step closer. "Once again, I have to say how grateful we are for the hospitality you've shown while I recovered. Your whole family has been kind and generous beyond anything I could have ever asked or expected. Without everyone's assistance, I might be dead."

As soon as the words left Jared's mouth, Rusty felt his heart turn cold. He couldn't imagine what would have happened without the Rios' generosity. It was unthinkable.

Maria reached out and touched Jared's hand. "You are more than welcome, Señor Gentry. I know you must be eager to get home to your new bride and that ranch you're building."

A smile spread across Jared's face. "Yes, ma'am, I sure am. It seems like I've been away from home a year instead of just a couple of months."

There was another knock, and Maria crossed the thick Spanish carpet and opened the door.

"Dr. Garcia! What a coincidence." She stood back and gestured for him to enter the room then extended her hand.

He took it, kissing the back softly. "Yes. As always, it's a pleasure to see you." He glanced at Jared. "I'm here to pay one last visit to my patient." His eyes returned to Maria. "And to give you a bit of unpleasant news." He laid his jacket and hat onto a chair. "Paulo Delgado is downstairs looking for Rachel. She's nowhere to be found, nor is Ana, for that matter. Paulo is raising the roof. I just left him shouting at poor Bonita because he can't find Rachel."

Maria threw her arms into the air. "I must go see what is happening." She turned to Jared. "Please join us for supper tonight. And you, too." She looked at Rusty. "If you're back from the mission in time."

Rusty shook his head. "Thank you, ma'am, but I'm going downstairs with you. I've seen Delgado's temper before, and I won't let you face him alone."

"No, Rusty. You get on out of here." Jared set one hand on his shoulder. "If you go down and confront Delgado, there's no telling what he'll do. It might even come to blows. I can handle him. If he's still ranting, I'll throw him out, sore ribs or no sore ribs."

"I can't let that happen. I'm going down with Señora Rios. You stay here and take care of yourself."

The three of them left the bedroom and started down the stairs.

When they reached the great room moments later, Paulo was nowhere in sight. Bonita knelt by an elaborately carved side table, collecting shards of a broken vase into her apron. She jumped at the sound of his boots on the hardwood floors, slicing her finger. Dr. Garcia flew to her side.

"Bonita," Maria snapped. "The doctor told me that Señor Delgado was here."

"He was, but he just left." Bonita paused and bit her lower lip. "He was furious when I mentioned Señorita Rios had gone before he arrived." She winced as the doctor applied pressure to her hand with the corner of her apron.

Rusty couldn't help interjecting his thoughts into the conversation. "So, he just broke the vase and stormed out?"

Bonita bobbed her head. "He said he was going to

look for her at the mission."

~

Rachel took a seat across from Father Antonio and folded her hands in her lap. The priest settled in behind a narrow desk in his sparse, unadorned office. "Ana is playing with the children on the back portico. It's well-shaded there and much cooler than the front." He gave her a warm smile. "She is such a sweet girl, and the children all adore her. She's a little ray of sunshine."

Rachel rolled her eyes. "Yes, sometimes a ray of sunshine and sometimes a little tornado." She looked down at her hands. "Father," she began slowly. "I need your counsel on a very personal matter."

His smile disappeared, and his eyes softened. "I can see that you're deeply troubled, Rachel. Please tell me what's made you so unhappy."

She sighed and lifted her eyes to meet his. "Padre, as you know, I am betrothed to Paulo Delgado."

He nodded. "Yes, I'll be the one to officiate at the wedding ceremony."

Rachel turned her head and gazed toward the window. "And the wedding rehearsal will be in two days." She turned back to him. "Father, I don't want to marry Paulo." She shook her head fervently. "I know this is what's expected of me, but when I think of spending the rest of my life with this man I don't love—a man that I have no respect for—it is almost unbearable to me." She swiped a tear from her cheek.

Father Antonio frowned. "My dear, I had no idea

you felt so strongly about this. I believe that arranged marriages are very common among the aristocratic landowners of our country. Have you told your Papá how unhappy you are with his choice of a husband for you?"

"Yes, many times. He says I'll learn to love Paulo. But I will not." Her voice became shrill, and she wrung her hands. "I don't want to be his wife."

Father Antonio tilted his head toward the window. "I believe Señor Rusty will be here to repair the bell tower for us today. He should be here soon." He leaned back in his chair and gave Rachel a knowing look. "This Rusty. Does he have anything to do with your distaste for Paulo?"

Rachel feigned indignance, then her face wilted. "Help me, Father. I simply cannot marry Paulo. I will never love him." She shook her head again. "This will break Papá's heart, but I've made up my mind. I will not marry Paulo."

Hoofbeats outside caused Rachel and the padre to hurry to the window. Rusty sat on his horse in the middle of the courtyard, scanning the area.

"It's Rusty—he's here to put up the new crossbeam for you."

Together they left the office and hurried downstairs and out the heavy oak mission doors, Father Antonio's long, black cassock blowing behind him. Rachel ran to Rusty's horse, gazing up at him with adoration.

"It's so good of you to come today just as you promised you would." The priest extended his hand to

Rusty in greeting.

Rachel agreed. "Yes, Father, and this is after he spent all day yesterday moving horses into the valley and slept on the ground in a bedroll last night."

Rusty held his hands up to stop her gushing praise. "It's nothin', Padre. I'm used to hard work and sleeping on the ground." He slid down from his horse, brushing against Rachel as he did so. "Well, I'd best get at this job before the day gets any hotter. Can you show me where the new crossbeam and ropes are? And I'll need a good ladder."

He turned back toward the arched entrance into the courtyard, stood stark still and squinted at the horizon.

"Señor Rusty?"

Rusty startled back to attention at the sound of his name. "Oh, I'm sorry, Father. What did you say?"

"Come with me. I'll show you where everything is."

Rusty led his mount to the shade of a tree and tethered him. He took a couple of steps forward and gazed into the distance again. Stopping in his tracks, he turned back to Father Antonio.

"Are you expecting visitors today? You've got two good-sized groups of riders coming from different directions, I'd guess they're about an hour out." He nodded toward the horizon. "One group from the south and one from just east of here, the way I came. They're riding fast and kicking up some dust."

Rachel moved in close to Rusty again, and Father

Antonio stepped in near his other side. His brow furrowed with concern.

"No, we never get more than a few visitors at a time, at least not since our truce with the Apache. I expect they're heading to Tubac, but I do find it odd to see two groups approaching at the same time."

"Well, I guess we'll soon find out what it's all about." Rusty led his horse to the shade under the eaves of the building and tethered him there. "I aim to keep my eyes on them, though. I don't feel easy about any of this."

~

Rusty climbed the steep staircase into the bell tower and set to work removing the old beam and ropes.

Some time later, he shouted down to the stone floor of the nave. "Miss Rachel, can you help me for a minute?"

She placed her walnut cookie on the saucer under her cup of tea and looked up. "Of course. I'll be right there." Rachel climbed the stairs to the bell tower, where Rusty was hard at work putting up the new ropes. In the heat of the small, warm space, he'd removed his shirt. He tightly held the hemp bell ropes, causing the muscles to flex taut in his broad shoulders and chest.

Suddenly remembering his state of undress, Rusty jerked, almost releasing the ropes. "I'm sorry, Miss Rachel! I was so wrapped up in what I was doing that I forgot to put my shirt on before I called you."

Rachel's eyes grew large and her cheeks flushed. "Oh…d-don't give it another thought, Señor Rusty," she stuttered, finally looking away. "You can't be expected to do such labor without becoming overheated."

Rusty considered releasing his grip on the ropes just to put his shirt on. "Could you help me out here for a minute, ma'am?"

Rachel drew near to him and looked up at his face. "Of course. What may I do to assist you?"

"Could you just take ahold of these new ropes and hold them steady? Try to keep them straight while I attach them to the new crossbeam and cut the old ones away. After that, I'll be done."

Rachel reached up and slid her hands over his. She maneuvered directly in front of him and leaned against his chest while they worked.

At that moment, without either of them having heard anyone approach, Paulo stepped into the tower, doubled his fist, and swung at Rusty.

Chapter Ten

Rusty grabbed Paulo's wrist the moment before it would have struck. He moved Rachel aside and shoved Paulo against the wall, pinning him flat. "You might think you have a problem with me, but you came mighty near to hitting Miss Rachel just now." He leaned in close.

Paulo's face twisted with anger. "How dare you put Rachel in such a compromising situation? If her father had seen you standing here half naked with his daughter… You should be horsewhipped for this. You know nothing about being a gentleman."

Rachel lurched at Paulo. "What on earth is wrong with you? I was simply helping Rusty with the bell ropes. Why must you assume something unsavory was going on?" She wedged herself between Rusty and Paulo and shouted at him. "You are the one who is no gentleman!"

Rusty released Paulo and stepped back a pace. "Don't explain yourself to him. He's determined to think the worst of things. Let him."

Paulo's face drew into a sneer. "Oh, it's clear to me

what is really happening here." He jutted his chin toward Rachel. "I'll deal with you about this once we're at your home."

Rusty grabbed him by the collar and drew him up an inch.

Father Antonio appeared in the doorway. "Stop it this instant! I will not tolerate this juvenile behavior here in the mission." He turned to Paulo. "This man was helping me by replacing the old crossbeam. He needed assistance from Rachel. You are mistaken if you think she would behave in anything but the most honorable way. Don't you know this young lady at all?"

Rusty backed away, grabbed his shirt, and shrugged it on.

Paulo scoffed. "Yes, I know her. But I also know this man is not to be trusted alone with Rachel."

Rusty tensed up as though he might come at Paulo again. "You're a funny one to talk about being trustworthy. Maybe you'd like to have a little conversation about the horses that have gone missing all over the valley."

Paulo narrowed his eyes, then growled at Rusty. "What is that supposed to mean?"

"You know *exactly* what I am talking about. Are you going to deny being involved in the horse rustling going on around the valley?"

Paulo barked a laugh. "Yes, I will deny it. Why would I need to be involved? I'm the son of a wealthy hacendado and about to become even richer through marriage."

Rachel gasped then her face reddened. "So, finally you admit your true motives."

Father Antonio stepped between them. "Please, Señor Delgado. I must ask you to leave."

Several horses galloping into the courtyard below sent the priest scurrying to the ledge of the tower. Rusty followed closely behind, buttoning his shirt.

He turned to Father Antonio. "It looks like the other group of riders has arrived."

A moment later, he watched as Paulo exited the mission and mounted his horse. The band of men who'd just ridden in blocked the gate, preventing him from leaving. The man who seemed to be in charge put his hand to his sidearm and moved his horse even closer to Paulo.

Rachel visibly tensed and whipped her head around, looking from Rusty to Father Antonio. "I believe one of those men is Jose Molina. He seems to be threatening Paulo."

Rusty turned and raced to the stairs, then stopped short. "Father, I left my pistol in my saddle bag, and my rifle is in its scabbard on my horse. I know this is a crazy question, but do you have a weapon of any kind?"

Father Antonio looked heavenward and whispered, "Forgive me." He scurried down the staircase, into his office, and opened the drawer to his desk. "We used to get a lot of banditos passing through on their way to Tubac, and it seems we have some here again."

He withdrew a pistol from the drawer and handed it to Rusty. "This is all I have, señor."

Rusty took the large, heavy, Colt Walker revolver, opened the cylinder, and checked the loads. His eyes widened as he gazed across the desk at the padre. He raised an eyebrow and lifted the corner of his mouth into a grin. "I reckon this'll do."

He started toward the front doors again, Rachel close at his heels and Father Antonio right behind her. Rusty stood back in the shadows and sized up the situation.

Rachel looked up at him with pleading eyes. "Even after the way Paulo has behaved here today, I'm afraid he's about to get killed." She placed her hand on Rusty's arm. "Please help him if you can."

"Of course, I'm gonna help him." Rusty cocked the gun and moved closer to the door. Rachel stayed fast at his heels. He whirled around and took her by the arm. "Oh, no you don't, missy. You're stayin' inside. Those are bad men out there and they're lookin' for trouble." He slid the enormous Colt into the back of his trousers and covered it with his shirttail. Firmly, he pushed Rachel further back into the room and stepped out into the courtyard.

About a dozen men turned Rusty's direction, none of them men he wanted to deal with. Still, he had to figure that, at least in this instance, Paulo was on his side.

He fixed his gaze on Paulo. "What seems to be the problem out here, Delgado?"

Paulo nodded to the scruffy band of riders. "This is Jose Molina. He frequently works for the Rodriguez family. It seems that he and his *compadres* have just come into some money and are looking to spend it in Tubac. They think they might find a few more pesos here at the mission."

Rusty took a couple of strides closer. "Is that so?"

Paulo pushed back his flat-brimmed hat, and it fell behind his shoulders. He pointed a thumb to a sweaty vaquero sitting his horse behind Molina. Rusty felt a wave of recognition. "Benito here tells me they've just sold some horses in Mexico, and they're on their way to the cantina in Tubac. But first, they want to have a word with Father Antonio." Paulo made eye contact with Rusty, his message clear. These men were horse rustlers.

Father Antonio trudged forward from behind Rusty. "Alright, what is it that you want? We have nothing here that would be of interest to you."

Molina shot an unpleasant smile over his shoulder. "Benito, go see if there is anything inside that we may be interested in."

As Benito dismounted and walked through the heavy, carved wooden doors, Ana scampered from the side of the building. She smiled, completely unaware of the tense events taking place in front of the mission.

"Well, well, well. Who is this little lovely?" A lecherous smile spread across Molina's ugly face.

Rachel flew out the door and grabbed Ana harshly by her arm.

Molina turned to his men and gestured for them to keep their guns on Paulo. Molina dismounted his palomino and started toward Ana and Rachel, his silver belt buckle gleaming in the sunlight. The band of men reeked of whiskey. Rusty could smell it from where he stood.

Rachel wrapped her arms around Ana and drew her close. "Please. She's only a little girl." She shoved Ana toward the doors. "Get back inside, Ana. Hide."

Molina laughed. "Well, she may be a little girl, but you most certainly are not."

Father Antonio lurched at Molina in an attempt to keep him away from the two girls. Molina slapped the priest to the ground and grabbed Rachel, pulling her against his chest, his arm crooked around her neck.

Rusty grabbed the pistol from his waistband and took aim at Molina. At the same time, his eyes fell on the silver belt buckle the man wore. Realization flooded him. This was the band of men who'd been stealing horses all over the valley.

Molina drew his gun on Rusty and Paulo. "Drop your weapons." Paulo let his gun fall to the ground and Rusty let the big Colt slip to his side. He was outnumbered and couldn't risk more harm to innocent bystanders.

Molina waved his pistol at them. "Get inside, all of you." Rusty and Father Antonio backed inside the mission, Paulo right behind them.

Molina mounted his horse and roughly pulled

Rachel up in front of himself in the saddle. He took one warning shot into the massive mission door, then spurred his horse through the gates and onto the road to Tubac.

~

Rusty threw the doors open and flew back outside. He snatched the Colt revolver from the ground and raced to his horse, mounting it with one rapid motion. The sound of the gunshot brought Paulo Delgado's men from behind the mission, where they'd been watering their horses in the shade of the back patio.

Within moments, Paulo emerged from the mission and mounted his horse, "I'll ride into Tubac and bring the law back with me. Rachel needs help."

Rusty sniggered and nodded. "You do that, Paulo. Go get some help." He laughed and shook his head as Paulo rode away.

Benito staggered out the mission door and to his horse. He looked at Rusty and said, "Perhaps you think you'll go to Señor Rios or my *patrón*, Señor Rodriguez." Benito laughed an unpleasant laugh. "I would not advise this. Not if you value your life." He drew his gun from his holster. Sweat dripped down the sides of his stubbly cheeks.

Rusty squinted at Benito, the gates behind him distorted by heat waves. "Oh, I won't go to your patrón or to Rios. You needn't worry about me." He smiled and raised his hands high. "In fact, now that you've robbed the alms box, why don't you follow your *amigo* Jose to Tubac and spend your ill-gotten gains?"

Benito snorted another laugh and swayed in his saddle. "You are amusing, señor. I've stolen nothing."

Rusty slowly walked his horse up close to the man. "Well…maybe I was mistaken, then. You seem like such a nice gent." Rusty extended a hand to Benito, who stared at it for a moment, then reached out his own hand.

At that moment, he grabbed Benito's arm and wrenched it, pulling him from his horse. Both men tumbled to the ground. Benito's gun fell impotently from his other hand. Rusty punched the dazed man, then pulled him up, twisting his arm behind his back.

"Padre, get his pistol." Rusty's shout stirred the stunned priest to life.

Father Antonio ran to the men and picked up Benito's gun.

"Get back inside, Father, and keep yourself and Miss Ana safe. I'm going after Rachel."

"Sí, you don't have to worry about Ana. I'd die before I let her come to any harm."

Rusty's lips lifted into the smallest of smiles. "Yes." He nodded. "I know you would."

Father Antonio scurried back into the mission, Benito's gun in one hand and the other on Ana's shoulder as he propelled her through the massive wooden doors.

"Okay, amigo, let's get you tied up so I can be on my way to Tubac."

Benito, seeming more sober, looked over his shoulder at Rusty. "Wait. I would like to make a deal with you."

Rusty shoved him toward his own horse and reached for a lariat.

"Wait, señor. I can help you get the girl away from Molina. I watched from the window as he took her away." He looked up at Rusty again and licked his lips. "Just listen. If you agree to let me ride away free after this is over, I can help you." He winced as Rusty shoved up on his twisted arm. "Believe me, Molina is not a man that you want to leave alone with a young woman." He laughed nervously. "You and your gun alone will not be enough to save the girl. You'll die trying."

Rusty shoved the man's arm up higher and tighter behind him. "Talk fast."

"Okay, okay, amigo." Benito gave a tense laugh. "Take me with you to the cantina in Tubac. I can get you there quickly." He chortled nervously again. "Then I'll go into the cantina and pretend I'm drunker than I really am. You'll be waiting outside, while I start a fight with one of Molina's men—you know—raise a commotion. Then when chaos breaks loose, you can make your move to free the lady."

"Look, I don't trust you, Benito, but right now, it seems like it might work." Rusty loosened his grip, slightly. "I'll have a gun aimed at your back every minute, so don't try anything stupid." He released the sweaty man and shoved him back a step.

"Yes, señor. You have my word."

Rusty waved Paulo's men forward, and Benito translated to them the plan they'd come up with. Within minutes the group of men pounded through the gates of the mission and onto the road to Tubac. A short time later, they pulled up in a small stand of mesquite trees behind Carmen's Cantina. They remained on their horses as Rusty and Benito rode near the establishment.

Rusty put a hand to his gun. "Okay, Benny. You go in and do exactly as we discussed. I'll be watching from the sidelines." Rusty donned a large sombrero he'd borrowed from one of the men and pulled it low, hoping to disguise his shock of auburn hair.

Benito staggered into the smoky, noisy cantina. Laughing and waving to the barkeep, he fell against the counter. "Drinks for everyone," he shouted above the din.

From the corner of the room, a guitar began to play a driving flamenco rhythm. A young woman jumped to her feet and whirled into the center of the room. Her arms raised gracefully, she stamped her feet in time with the music, her castanets clacking furiously. Spinning like a top, her full, ruffled skirts swirled around her as she danced.

Rusty pulled his sombrero lower and entered the cantina. He kept his head down as he slinked to a dark corner near the door and slid low into a chair. His eyes quickly found Rachel, who Molina held fast on his lap, his filthy hands wandering much too near forbidden places on her body.

She pushed Molina's sweaty face away and slashed at it with her nails. A bright red streak appeared on his cheek. He grabbed her hair, jerked her head back, and raised his hand, threatening to slap her face. Instead, he broke into a loud, nasty laugh. Molina pressed his mouth to hers, but Rachel turned away, a look of disgust on her face. She pulled an arm free from his grasp and rammed an elbow into his ribs.

The look of revulsion and sheer terror on Rachel's face tore at Rusty's heart. He raised up a couple of inches in his chair, then forced himself to sit back down. Attacking Molina now would only get him killed and put Rachel in further danger. *I'll get my chance.*

He sat back and took stock of the men in the room. Benito continued his drinking and revelry, interacting with the crowd. Molina's men guzzled their free tequila, getting drunker by the minute.

As Rusty watched and waited for Benito to start a brawl, a familiar face stepped from the shadows. Carlos Rodriguez sidled up to Molina and pulled Rachel from his lap.

Once again, Rusty raised himself from his chair and put a hand to his gun, but before he could make his move, Carlos laughed and slapped Molina on the back.

"Well, Jose, I see you've finally made it here. I was afraid you'd started for Mexico City with my share of the money!"

"Do not worry. I have your money, Carlos. The horses we removed from Señor Rios's herd were valuable, and we got a good price when we sold them."

An anonymous hand grabbed Rachel and pulled her farther away from Molina, who snarled. "Hey, that one is mine!"

"We're only going to dance, patrón."

Rachel shuddered and turned her head away.

Rusty couldn't stand it for another moment. He slammed his chair back against the wall and charged the drunken bandit that held Rachel in his grasp.

Picking up a chair, Benito smashed it across a nearby man's back.

Just as predicted, chaos broke out in the cantina. The dancer squealed and ran to the wall, the music stopped, and the musician made a hasty retreat up the staircase at the rear of the room.

Rachel's fists came up, and she pummeled the man's chest with all her might. "Let me go, you filthy animal!" She struggled against him, kicking.

Rusty stepped in and grabbed both her wrists. "Rachel, it's me. Run outside!" He shoved her toward the door. He drew a fist back at the drunken man who'd held her in his sweaty grasp, landing a jaw-busting punch into his face. Molina grabbed Rusty by the back of his collar and spun him around, pounding him back into one of the cantina's tables.

Rusty thrust both legs out and made contact with Molina's chest, sending him flying across the room. The bandito behind him pulled Rusty up by his shirt and attempted to hit him again, but Rusty blocked his blow. He recoiled and threw a punch to the man's nose. He heard a cracking sound as it made contact.

From out of nowhere, Molina jumped Rusty's back,

wrapping his arms around his shoulders. The stench of his sweaty, unwashed body assaulted Rusty's nose. He bent forward and threw Molina over his shoulder, hurtling him across the room. Rusty lunged at Molina again, grabbed him by his shirt and the seat of his pants, and sent him flying to the back of the room.

Rachel's shouting reached Rusty's ears. He ran out the door to her and pulled her close. Sobbing with relief, she threw her arms around his neck. "*Madre de Dios. Please get me out of here,*" she said.

Benito exited the cantina and turned to Rusty. They made eye contact and Rusty jerked his head toward the tethered horses. "Go."

Rusty grabbed Rachel by her arm and led her around the side of the adobe and toward his horse. As he stepped into the saddle and reached down for Rachel, hooves pounded up beside them. Paulo jumped down from his horse, jerked Rachel around by her shoulder and shook her.

"Again, Rachel? How many times must I find you in the arms of this *Americano?*" Before he could get another word from his mouth, Rusty leapt off his horse, pulled Paulo away from Rachel, drew back, and sent him flying against the nearby trees.

"Don't you ever lay a hand on her! Do you hear me? I'll take you apart if you ever raise a hand to her again." Rusty lunged for him, as the deputy sheriff from Tubac reined in beside the little group and jumped down from his mount.

"Break it up. Now!" he shouted. The deputy ran to Rusty and pulled him off Paulo, who sat up and pressed a hand to his bleeding mouth. "Paulo, is this the bandito you told me about?" Paulo stared daggers at Rusty and didn't answer.

Rachel ran to Rusty and wrapped her arms around his waist. "No, deputy. This is the man who rescued me from Jose Molina. Jose forced me to come here against my will." She looked up into his face. "Señor Cunningham helped me escape."

Paulo climbed to his feet and took one faltering step forward. He shook a finger at Rusty. "You think you've won, 'Rusty.'" He said his name with a sneer. "But you have not. Rachel is my fiancée, and our wedding will take place exactly as planned."

Rusty smiled and put a hand to Rachel's back. "Well, you may be right, Señor Delgado. She's your fiancée, but if she was mine, I'd show her every day how beautiful and special she is, not yell threats at her." He pushed a lock of hair back from her face. "Right now, I'm taking Rachel back to the mission to check on her sister and Father Antonio."

He turned his attention to the deputy who stood beside Paulo. "I think the men you're looking for are inside the cantina, breaking the place to pieces." He looked down at Rachel and led her to his horse. "Come on, Rachel." He looked pointedly at Paulo. "Let me get you and Miss Ana home."

Rusty mounted his horse and pulled Rachel up

behind him in the saddle. She wrapped her arms around his waist and rested her head on his shoulder. Exhausted, she closed her eyes. Rusty gazed down at Paulo, nodded to him, smiled, and nudged the sides of his horse.

The heavy doors to the mission swung open as Rusty galloped through the iron gates and into the courtyard. His lips widened into a grin when Ana, followed by Father Antonio, stepped out into the hot sunshine. Ana raced up to Rusty's horse and reached out to Rachel. "Thank God you're okay, my sister." Rachel clasped Ana's outstretched hand.

Father Antonio hurried to Ana's side and helped Rachel down from the horse. "We've been praying for you both to return to us safely. Yes, thank God you're unharmed."

Rusty dismounted. "Padre, I'm purely sorry this all happened. I did get the repair finished on the bell, though. I think it will last you another twenty years now."

Father Antonio shook his head. "Please. Don't say you're sorry. If you hadn't been here when those bandits rode in—well, I can't bear to think of what might have happened to these two girls."

Rachel gently touched the priest's face. "Father, are you sure you're alright? Do you need to see a doctor?"

"Oh, no, no, no." He brushed off the idea. "It's nothing but a bruise." He laughed. "I used to get worse wrestling with my brothers when we were boys."

Father Antonio slapped Rusty lightly on the shoulder. "Thank you, my son. God knows you've done more today than any man should have to do."

Rusty extended his hand to the priest. "It was my pleasure, Padre."

He looked at the Rios sisters and smiled. "I think I'd better get you two home before a search party comes looking for you." He steered them toward Rachel's carriage that stood parked in the shade.

He turned back to Father Antonio. "Oh, by the way. The deputy from Tubac has Molina and his bunch of horse thieves under arrest by this time. So, if you find anything missing from the church, be sure and let him know. I figure he'll find it in the possession of one of those men."

Rusty took Ana's hand and assisted her into the carriage. He tied his horse to the back of the buggy and faced Rachel. "Bring your canteens to the well. We've got a long, hot ride ahead of us."

Cool water splashed down the side of the stone well as he filled his canteen from the bucket. Rachel opened hers, waiting for the cold liquid. He turned to her. "Rachel, I don't know what I would have done if one of those men had harmed you." He closed his eyes against the thought. "I prayed more today than I've ever prayed in my life."

She stroked his cheek. "But I am okay, and it's because of you."

He bent down and pulled her to his chest. "Rachel," he breathed into her ear, his voice a hoarse whisper. He pressed her head back and kissed her with an intensity that frightened him. He felt the breath go out of her, then begin again in ragged puffs.

He backed away from her, one short step, and took the other canteen that still dangled by its strap from her arm. "Let me get you and Miss Ana home to your family. You still got a mighty unpleasant conversation to have with your papá."

Chapter Eleven

Rusty tied his mount to the rear of Rachel's carriage, took the driver's seat beside the two girls, and slapped the reins. Despite the heat, Rachel sat near him, her side pressed close to his. Occasionally, she reached over and gently caressed his arm.

He spoke softly to her. "Are you sure you're okay, Rachel? They didn't really hurt you, did they?" He looked over at Ana. "And are you alright? That must have been a terrifying experience for you, too."

Rachel lifted her eyes to him. "Yes, I'm fine. But if you had not shown up when you did…" She shuddered and rubbed goosebumps from her arms.

Ana took Rachel's hand. "Me, too, Señor Rusty. None of those men touched me. But poor Father Antonio. He has a large bruise on his face from that filthy brute who struck him down."

Rusty grimaced at the thought of all that had transpired. "I just thank the good Lord nothing worse happened." He looked at the two girls beside him. "But that bunch are all locked up tight in the Tubac jail now.

And I made sure the marshal knows that Molina was involved in the horse rustling that's been going on around the valley. Carlos Rodriguez was a part of it, too. He's the one that tipped Molina off about the herd we drove into new pasture last night." Rusty shook his head. "It's hard to believe so much has happened since yesterday morning. And the day ain't even over yet. We still have to tell your Papá about everything that took place."

Ana leaned forward and raised her voice. "Oh no, Señor Rusty! We don't need to tell Papá about any of this. He'll never let me leave the hacienda again. He may even lock me in my room."

Rachel laughed. "Perhaps you *should* be locked in your room, Ana. If you recall, I didn't want you to come with me today. You're a very impetuous girl, my little sister."

Ana stiffened her back. "I'm impetuous? You risked riding alone into the desert and facing banditos, just for a chance to be alone with Señor Rusty."

"Ana!" Rachel gasped and turned an embarrassed face to Rusty, who kept his eyes on the road. But a tiny smile of satisfaction lifted the corners of his mouth.

"Well, it's true, isn't it?" Ana folded her arms and huffed. "I'm hungry, and it's so hot."

"I knew this would happen." Rachel elbowed Ana lightly. "You can never make this trip to the mission without complaining, yet you always insist on coming."

She reached behind the seat and retrieved the

saddlebags Rosa had prepared early that morning. "Cook packed a little food for me to bring. I don't know what it is, but we can share it."

Rusty reined into a shady copse of trees. "Let's take a break, and then we'll go on the rest of the way." He came around the buggy and helped both girls down. "Don't wander off, Miss Ana. There could be a rattler under any of these trees."

"I won't. I've had all the excitement I want for a very long time."

~

Rachel passed out the small lunch and they ate, washing it down with water from their canteens.

"Excuse me." Ana gave a shy look. "I must walk over there for a few moments." She pointed to a stand of creosote bushes. "I'll be back shortly."

Rachel and Rusty strolled to the carriage. She faced him and touched his forearms, waiting for him to lift her to the seat as he'd done so many times. Instead, he hesitated, then unbuttoned his shirt pocket. He pulled out a thin, silver bracelet inlaid with turquoise stones.

"I know it ain't much, but when I saw it at the General Store in Nogales, I thought of you." He shrugged and lowered his eyes. "I knew you were promised to another man, and I couldn't give it to you, but I figured I'd keep it as a reminder of my time with you."

She gasped in surprise. Tears welled up in her eyes. "For me, Rusty?" She felt as though she were looking at one of the crown jewels of England. She extended her hand so he could place it on her arm.

Rusty fastened it around her tiny wrist, lifted her fingers to his lips, and kissed them tenderly.

"Thank you, Rusty. I'll treasure this forever." She wrapped her arms around him and rested her head on his shoulder.

He held her close, then sighed sharply and pushed her back to arm's length. "Rachel, we have to stop this. We both know it can never be—there's no future for us." He looked away from her. "You don't even really know me."

"What do you mean I don't know you?" She turned his face to her and gazed into his eyes. "I know you're the kindest, most loyal man I've ever met—a man who would die for a friend. A strong, hard-working man, who asks for nothing in return."

She stroked his cheek. "I know that the moment you come into my presence, I can feel the power of your nearness. I want to reach over and take your hand whenever you're beside me. And that your face is the first one that comes into my mind every morning when I open my eyes." She laid his hand on her cheek. Her voice broke as she spoke to him. "I know that the thought of never seeing you again causes me terrible pain."

She lifted her eyes. "Yes, you come from a humble background. Why do you think this would matter to me, Rusty?" Her voice grew stronger. "Don't you know it only makes me admire you more? My grandfather came to this country with only a few pesos in his pocket. He built the beginnings of a great ranchero from nothing. My father, also a humble man, brought it the rest of the way to the greatness you see now." She touched his arm. "I see these same qualities in you, Rusty Cunningham. That's only one of the reasons I reject Paulo. He wants only what is given to him and to spend money on his own pleasure. I know you're a different kind of man." She squeezed his hand. "Yes, I do know you."

Rusty turned away from her attempting to hide the tears stinging his eyes. "Rachel. I…I don't know what to say to you right now."

"Do you love me, Rusty?"

He shook his head. "Don't ask me that."

She turned him toward her. "Yes, I must ask it. Do you love me?"

He pulled her so close she could barely breathe, lifted her face to his, and pressed his lips to hers. She could feel his deep love and passion pour into her. Finally, he put his lips to her ear. "Yes, I love you, Rachel. You've ruined me forever. I'll never love another woman now but you. I'll love you till I draw my last breath. But…"

She stopped him short. "No, there is no 'but.' I won't live my life with a man I care nothing for. You, Rusty… I only want you. I'll tell Papá today. I refuse to marry Paulo, no matter the consequences to me."

Rusty took her shoulders and searched her eyes. "Could it be possible? Could we find a way to be together?"

"Yes, Rusty. We can find a way if it's what we both want."

He hung his head then looked off into the distance. "Rachel, you were born into wealth and luxury. Raised with everything a girl could want. You've never experienced the kind of life you'd live with me." He looked into her eyes. "I'm afraid the reality of it would be too much of a shock for you."

"Do you really think I'm so shallow?" Rachel scowled. "I know the harsh reality of being poor. Why do you think I spend so much time with the orphans at the mission? Money means nothing to me except an opportunity to help those in need." She touched his stubbly cheek. "I'd rather be poor with the man I love than wealthy with someone I care nothing for."

A smile tugged at the corners of his lips. He inhaled and blew out a long breath. "I do have a little money saved—enough to get us started with a small spread. With a lot of hard work, we could have a decent little ranch for ourselves." He searched her face. "Are you sure, Rachel? Really sure this is what you want?"

She bounced up onto her tiptoes and threw her arms around his neck again. "Yes, Rusty. I am so sure!"

He planted another quick kiss on her lips and hugged her tight. "If you want me, girl, you've got me."

Ana bustled up to the carriage. "Okay, I'm ready

to go now." She gazed from Rachel's face to Rusty's, her eyes wide. "What's wrong with you two?"

Chapter Twelve

Rusty flew into the house and was halfway up the stairs before Jared called out to him. "Whoa there, buddy. Where's the fire?"

Rusty stopped so fast, he almost lost his balance. "I was just on my way to talk to you." He turned and sprinted down the stairs again.

Jared leaned against the doorjamb of the great room. He held a glass of cold tea, a drink that the cook had kindly begun preparing for the two men during their stay at the hacienda.

Rusty dashed past Jared and nabbed his glass as he flew by. "Thank you, pal—I'm bone dry."

Jared's mouth dropped open as Rusty guzzled half the goblet of tea and then plopped into a nearby chair. Jared cocked an eyebrow. "Okay, I'm almost afraid to ask. Is this good mood of yours because we're heading home tomorrow, or is it for some other reason? Possibly one that has big brown eyes and smells like honeysuckle?"

Rusty chuckled, pitched his hat onto the sofa, and

ruffled his mane of trail-dusty hair. "Now, where would you get an idea like that?"

"Hmm. Well, I know why *I'm* eager to get out of here, but I can't figure out what's got you in such a lather."

Rusty sat forward and leaned his elbows on his knees. "Sit down. I do need to talk to you."

Jared sighed and took the chair opposite him. "I knew it. What's going on?"

Rusty glanced toward the doorway, remembering Teresa and her eavesdropping from before. He looked down and then peered up at Jared, grinning. "Alright, something did happen. Rachel and Ana were at the mission this morning when I went to work on the bell tower." He leaned back in his chair, shook his head, and threw his hands in the air. "Man, I don't even know where to begin. We had a week's worth of things happen today, but the upshot is that Rachel is calling off her engagement to Delgado."

Jared stared at Rusty, his expression incredulous. "And?"

Rusty blew out a slow breath. "And—me and Rachel want to be together." He shrugged. "I don't know yet how that's gonna happen, but we sure plan to try." He peered at Jared, knowing he must think he'd lost his mind.

Jared sat motionless, his eyes wide in amazement. "So…you're serious about this? Both of you?"

"Serious as a sharp stick in the eye."

Jared dropped back in his chair and exhaled. "Wow! I was expecting something of a surprise, but this has left me at a loss for words."

Rusty gave a sheepish grin.

"So, I guess you'll be staying here in Sonora?"

"We haven't talked about that yet, but it's a possibility. If it works out that I stay, I'll ride to Tucson with you and see you on your way back to Missouri."

Jared held up a hand. "That wouldn't be necessary."

"No, I won't hear any argument about it. I understand the stage to Kansas City only comes through there once a week, and I want to make sure you're settled and have everything in order before I ride away."

Jared hung his head. "I'm happy for you, buddy. I'm sure you've thought this through." It was more a question than a statement. He looked up into Rusty's face and extended his hand. "It's gonna be a huge loss to leave you behind, but I wish you every happiness."

Rusty grasped his friend's hand. "Thank you. But who knows? Rachel might decide to go back with me until things settle down here with her father and Delgado. We'll see how this all shakes out."

Jared stood and made his way to the side table. "Well, this calls for a toast, my friend." He found another glass and poured more tea for both of them. He handed Rusty's to him and lifted his drink. "To the best friend and trail partner a man ever had. Here's to you and Miss Rachel. May you have a lifetime of happiness."

Rusty clinked his cup to Jared's and raised it to his lips. He heard lilting laughter coming from the next room and wondered if Rachel had come in. She'd have the devil to pay when her father found out she left the rancho without telling anyone but Bonita—and had taken Ana with her.

Rusty turned and strode through the door into the foyer, Jared right behind him. Dr. Garcia's hearty laugh mingled with Maria Rios'.

Maria directed her attention to Jared. "Ah, Señor Gentry, it's good to see you out of your room." She smiled warmly and stepped closer.

"Yes." Dr. Garcia spoke to Jared but immediately turned his gaze back to Maria. "I'm also pleased to see you downstairs and moving about. You need to exercise to regain your strength after being inactive for so long."

Jared shrugged. "I plan to keep busy today. I have a lot to do. Rusty and I have a long ride ahead of us when we go home."

Dr. Garcia's expression became serious. "So, you plan to start for home soon? I hope you don't intend to go such a great distance by horseback?"

"No, we sent our personal mounts home with the herd. We'll borrow horses from Señor Rios and ride to Tucson, then take the stagecoach on to Kansas City."

Rusty chuckled. "I'd never let him make that long trip on horseback."

Dr. Garcia touched Jared on his shoulder and smiled. "I'm happy to hear that. I believe it's a wise decision."

They walked back into the great room, and Maria went to the window. "Where is Rachel…the rebellious girl? When my brother learns of this, he'll be furious."

Rusty cleared his throat and shot a glance at Jared. "Actually, she's here somewhere. She rode back with me from the mission."

Dr. Garcia came to stand beside Maria. "Come, I will help you look for her."

Maria nodded her agreement. "Yes, let's start looking by the fountain. She loves it there." She turned to Rusty and Jared. "Please make yourselves comfortable. I'll send Bonita in to see if you need anything."

Rusty watched Señora Rios and Dr. Garcia as they strode out the door and onto the shaded colonnade. They slowed their gait to a stroll, and Dr. Garcia bent his head close to Maria's ear. She slipped her arm through his, and Rusty heard her light laughter again. He grinned. It seemed love could bloom at any age. He smiled to see the serious and sometimes severe Maria behaving like a young girl in love. Rusty sighed and gazed at the distant horizon. *Soon, Rachel…soon you and I will be man and wife and begin a life together.*

~

With the evening meal over, Rachel gathered her courage for the unpleasant task ahead. She straightened her back, took a deep breath, and strode to the great room door. A peek inside showed her family sitting together in relaxed conversation. Papá and Tía Maria sipped their brandy, and Teresa and Ana held glasses of cold lemonade.

Rachel smoothed the skirt of her pale blue dress and whispered a prayer for the strength to do what she needed to. She crossed the threshold and timidly paced across the deep green patterned carpet.

Papá gave a tight smile as she approached him. She fearfully peeked up at his face and saw the slow burning anger in his eyes. "Ah, Rachel, *mijita*. Come and join us." He extended a hand to her. Guilt and apprehension filled her as she sat next to him on the cushioned sofa. This wouldn't be an easy task.

"Thank you, Papá." She sat ramrod straight on the edge of the cushion and nervously looked at the people seated around the room. Rachel cleared her throat and fidgeted with her bracelet, twisting it and rubbing the turquoise stones.

"Papá."

"Yes, my dear."

She cleared her throat again.

Domingo stood up and paced to the table where crystal decanters holding various wines and imported liquors sat. He selected one and held it up to the light. "Our own wine. I believe this is a vintage from eight years ago." He poured it into his glass and took a sip. "Ahhh… excellent. Our grapes are unsurpassed, if I do say so myself." He selected a fragrant cigar from the humidor and waved it under his nose. He shot Rachel a pointed look. She could see he would not make this easy for her.

Tía Maria sat up straighter and firmly plunked her goblet on the table. "Domingo, you know Dr. Garcia said you're not to smoke those things anymore."

He frowned, sniffed it again, and placed it back in the humidor.

He turned once more to Rachel. "My daughter, I heard you had a very eventful day."

She looked at Ana, then Tía Maria, and then squared her shoulders. "Yes, Papá. I'm very sorry that I didn't speak with anyone about my visit to the mission. I could not find you or Tía Maria at the time." Her eyes darted to Ana, who looked out the window. "And there is something important that I need to say to you."

She heard Ana's sharp intake of breath, and then Papá waved an arm impatiently. "Well, what is this important thing you want to say?"

Rachel's voice came out a tiny squeak. "Papá…" She cleared her throat yet again and blurted out the words. "Papá, I have decided that I will not marry Paulo. I don't love him. I could never be happy with him and don't want to be his wife." She peered up at her father and saw his face frozen with shock and confusion. "I don't even like Paulo. I'm sorry, Papá, but I *won't* marry him."

Tía Maria threw a hand to her bosom. A small,

strangled shriek came from Teresa's throat, and she looked at Rachel in disbelief. Ana scooted to the front of her chair and giggled nervously.

Papá looked around the room from face to face as if waiting for someone to tell him this was all a bad joke, but no one did. He sputtered and stammered. "What…what is this? This can't be true. Surely you jest." He clumsily sat his glass on the table. It tipped over, spilling wine onto the thick carpet. "This is all arranged, Rachel. I've selected Paulo as your husband." His voice grew louder, and his face redder. He roared, "You *will* marry him in four days, exactly as planned!"

Rachel began to tremble, then felt determination well up inside her. "No, Papá. I'm sorry, but I won't. I have no wish to hurt you, but I'm not going to marry Paulo."

Domingo took one lumbering step forward and fell into his chair. He clutched the left side of his chest and clawed at his shirt, gasping for air.

Chapter Thirteen

Rachel sat stunned. She stared at her father as his face grew ghastly pale and sweaty. His eyes bulged.

Roused from her shock, Rachel jumped to her feet and ran to him. "Papá …Papá!" She dropped to her knees beside him and took his free hand, patting it.

"Ana, run and get Dr. Garcia. He's still here, tending to Bonita in the servants' quarters. Hurry!"

Tía Maria ran to her brother's side and frantically waved her fan in his face.

Rachel loosened his tie and opened the top button of his shirt.

He gasped for air and dropped his head against the back of the chair.

Tía Maria crossed herself and whispered a prayer.

Teresa stood slowly and took a step toward Rachel. She spoke through clenched teeth. "Well, my sister, I hope you're happy now." Her face contorted in anger, and she shouted her angry words. "You may have killed our Papá in your determination to have your way."

Rachel turned to Teresa, her mouth agape. "I…I."

She turned back to her father. "Papá, I'm so sorry. Please be okay." In her despair, she impulsively blurted out. "I'll marry Paulo if that will make you happy."

Dr. Garcia bustled into the room and dropped his medical bag at Domingo's feet. "Everyone, stand back. Give him air."

Tía Maria backed up a step, then turned to Dr. Garcia. "Eduardo, help him." She twisted her hands. "Is it his heart?"

"I need everyone to leave this room at once so I can examine Domingo." He furrowed his brow and turned to Tía Maria. "Please, Maria," he said more gently. "I'll come out and speak to you as soon as I'm able." He nodded toward the door. "And close the door behind you."

Tía Maria huffed, then did as he asked. She put an arm around Rachel and led her nieces out of the room, closing the door after them.

In the vast foyer outside the great room, the women huddled in disbelief at what had occurred. Rachel wrung her hands and began to pace. "Oh, Papá, I'm so sorry. I never meant for such a terrible thing to happen." But the thought of the promise she'd just made—a promise to marry Paulo, nearly drove her to despair. In a single moment, she'd undone everything she set out to do—break her engagement to Paulo. *Dear Lord, how will I get myself out of this?*

Teresa whirled around on her sister, her black

eyes snapping. "You *should* be sorry, Rachel." She spat the words. "Ever since you met this gringo cowboy, you've been defiant." She jutted her chin for emphasis. "You are infatuated with him, and in your selfish rebellion, you may have killed our Papá."

Ana raced to Rachel's side and threw her arms around her waist. "You stop speaking to Rachel that way!" She began to sob, and Rachel wrapped her younger sister in a hug.

"It's okay, dear. I have been selfish." She rested her head on Ana's. "I never dreamed such a thing as this would happen."

Maria stood near Teresa and raised her hands to still the argument. "Girls, please stop this. It will not help your Papá now. We must pray to our heavenly Father for his recovery."

Teresa swiped angry tears from her cheeks. "Yes, you're right, Tía. But when I think of the injustice to Paulo, it breaks my heart." She wiped another tear. "He is a good man and doesn't deserve such treatment." She glared at Rachel and turned her back.

"Why do you care so much, Teresa?" Rachel leaned toward her sister, her face tense, eyes burning. "Paulo is self-centered and always angry about something. And yet you defend him at every turn."

"You don't understand him." Teresa shook her head slowly. "It saddens me that you have no inkling of what lies within the heart of this man you're engaged to." She wrinkled her nose. "Don't you know that Paulo is a traditional man? That he loves the land and desires only to carry on the traditions of our forefathers? He puts honor and family before himself?"

Rachel couldn't hold back a snort. "Are you speaking of the same Paulo who shouted at Bonita earlier?"

Teresa shrugged. "Clearly you don't see or appreciate these qualities, but I know Paulo's heart. You, on the other hand, seem to enjoy rousing his anger and bringing out the very worst in him."

Tía Maria raised her voice. "Girls, enough! Your arguing only makes things worse." She pulled the weeping Ana to her side. "Don't cry, my sweet. Dr. Garcia will take good care of your papá. It will all be okay…it must be." Maria raised her eyes heavenward.

When the doors to the great room opened, Dr. Garcia stepped out into the foyer and took Maria's hand. The girls gathered around him.

"How is Papá?" Rachel asked.

Dr. Garcia pinched the bridge of his nose. "He will be okay. I don't believe it was his heart, but a severe attack of anxiety, brought on by the shock of your argument."

Rachel threw her hands to her face and looked at Tía Maria. "This is such good news."

Voices tumbled over each other, all saying how grateful they were that Domingo would be okay.

Dr. Garcia held up a hand. "But…" He glanced from face to face. "He must stay calm. He was lucky today, but if there is a next time, the stress could bring on a worse episode with his heart." He shook his head. "Domingo is a strong man, but with his volatile temperament, the cigars, and his refusal to slow down in his hard work—well, it's just better not to allow him to become so upset." He touched Maria gently on her back. "Now, I must get your brother to his room. I'll give him a mild sedative so he'll rest for a while."

Rachel watched the doctor walk away. She sighed, strolled to the window, and stared toward the red dirt road leading to the hacienda. Rusty had ridden up that path earlier this evening. She'd told him that she loved him and would break her engagement to Paulo. A short time ago, in her effort to appease her father, she'd told him she would marry Paulo. Clouds gathered above the mesa. *Yes, a storm is brewing. Lord, please help me. I don't know which way to turn right now. I don't think I can bear to see Rusty ride away from me. But how can I endanger my Papá's life?*

~

As the shadows lengthened across the terracotta tiles of the patio, Rachel arose from her seat by the splashing fountain. She filled a vase with red zinnias from the flowerpots bordering the court. These would cheer Papá.

Upstairs, she raised her hand to tap on the door of his bedroom, but before she could knock, Dr. Garcia opened it and stepped into the hallway.

"Rachel, your father is resting comfortably now.

Your Tía Maria is sitting with him." Dr. Garcia touched her arm. "Please don't stay too long. I want Domingo to sleep for the rest of the evening. I'll check on him in the morning."

"Of course, doctor. I'll only stay a moment. I want to tell him goodnight."

Rachel slipped into the room and took a few quiet paces in the direction of her father's bed. The great mahogany wardrobe near the door blocked her view of Papá and Tía Maria, but she could hear their voices. She tiptoed forward until they came into view.

"Maria, please don't remind me of those unhappy memories of so long ago. I know you fled to Spain rather than marry Felipe." He dropped his head back on the pillow. "And now, after all these years, you remain unmarried."

Maria arose from the chair beside Domingo's bed and folded her hands at her waist. She exhaled deeply. "I'm sorry, I don't want to upset you. I'll change the subject." She ambled to the deep-set window. "Would you like me to open this for you? The clouds are blowing rapidly over Tumacácori mesa. Perhaps you'll get a breeze in your room."

Domingo pulled himself up higher on his pillows. "Yes, Maria. That would be nice."

She turned the handle, pushed the glass pane forward, and inhaled deeply. "Oh, yes—this is lovely." She stood gazing into the gathering darkness. "I can see just the corner of your vineyards from here." She looked back at him. "No wonder you love the view from this room so much."

Domingo smoothed his blanket. "Yes, this is the best view in the *casa*. This is why my beloved wife chose it for us so many years ago." A wistful look crossed his face. "One can see everything from here. The vineyard, the mesas, and the remuda."

Rachel silently shifted her weight, careful to stay in the shadows.

Domingo turned to Maria. "Speaking of the vineyards, would you fetch me a small glass of brandy?"

Maria snapped around. "Don't be ridiculous! Only hours ago, you had a terrible nervous episode, and you want me to bring you brandy?"

He lifted his shoulders in a sheepish shrug. "Well, Dr. Garcia did say that I was to rest and stay calm."

"Yes, and you will remain calm without the aid of brandy." She stiffened her spine and turned back to the window.

Domingo curled his lips into the smallest smile. "Dr. Garcia. He spends an unusually large amount of time here lately. And not just because of our wounded American cowboy or Bonita's cut hand. So many dinners. So many strolls on the portico."

Maria paced back to the chair and sat down. She raised her eyebrows. "Yes, he has been here a lot, hasn't he?"

"Is there maybe something here that holds his

interest? Or someone?" He gestured toward Maria.

She tilted her head. "Perhaps there is." She sighed. "You know, my brother, life is better—the air smells sweeter, and the sun shines brighter when one has a love to stroll with."

She lifted her eyes and peered into the shadows, straight at Rachel. "You may not realize it, Domingo, but you have a daughter who is very much in love."

He whipped his head toward Maria. "If you mean Rachel and Señor Cunningham, I am aware." He waved off the idea. "Rusty is a good man, I think, but the infatuation between those two is doomed." He jerked his blanket up for emphasis.

"No, I'm not speaking of Rachel." She spoke slowly and deliberately. "I mean your daughter Teresa." She leaned toward him and crooked a brow. "Teresa is very much in love with Paulo." Maria stood up and walked to the lamp. She removed the blue cut-glass shade, struck a match, and lit the wick. "It's getting dark in here. I'll turn the flame low so you can rest."

Domingo sat up straight. "One moment, my sister." His voice was remarkably strong. "What do you mean, Teresa is in love with Paulo?"

Maria shrugged. "She simply is." She replaced the globe on the lamp. "You haven't seen the looks Teresa gives Paulo, and heard the things she says to him." Maria returned to his bedside and sat down again. "You may want to consider that you've matched Paulo to the wrong daughter." She peered at him. "You know, you could still fulfill your dream for the future of your empire through Teresa and Paulo. This is something for you to think about." She twisted a lock of hair. "If Rachel marries Paulo, Teresa will spend years—maybe her whole life, in love with her sister's husband."

Domingo crossed his arms. "Why must you women constantly interfere?" he thundered. "Rachel is betrothed to Paulo. She is the eldest daughter. This is the marriage that will take place."

Maria exhaled slowly, stood, then bent down and kissed Domingo on the forehead. "Rest well, my brother." She strode to the deeply shaded corner, where she came face to face with her niece. Rachel clutched the vase of flowers to her chest and took a step back. Maria nodded toward the door, and they exited the room together.

Chapter Fourteen

After breakfast, Rachel sat on the patio, basking in the golden light of the desert morning. She held an open book in her lap. She tried to read, but couldn't focus. As she stared out through the open gate, Rachel relived two scenes over and over. Rusty when he told her yesterday that he loved her. And Papá as he fell into his chair when she said she wouldn't marry Paulo. She still hadn't talked to Rusty since their ride home from the mission. He hadn't come downstairs for supper last night or breakfast this morning. He must be waiting for her to tell him how her talk with Papá had gone. Her mind raced in wild circles as she tried to decide how to handle things. Dr. Garcia had said another attack of stress like yesterday might kill Papá. She gazed through the wrought iron gates into the distance and prayed.

Behind her, she heard the rapid click of steps coming toward her. Instantly, she knew it was Paulo. Rusty's footsteps were much different, with his long, steady gait. She steeled herself for another unpleasant tirade from Paulo.

Paulo stood before her, and without the benefit of any greeting or small talk, he got right to the point. "Rachel, I've just come from speaking to your father. He now knows about everything that took place yesterday, and he agrees with me that the sooner this marriage takes place, the better."

Rachel jumped up, letting her book fall to the ground. "Paulo, how could you? Dr. Garcia said Papá isn't to be upset! Don't you know about the episode he had yesterday?"

He bobbed his head rapidly. "Oh, yes." His eyes blazed. "Oh, yes. I know about it, my dear." He began to pace. "Señor Rios informed me that you attempted to call off our wedding. How very kind of you, Rachel. It was quite a shock to learn this from your father."

She hung her head. "I'm sorry you had to learn it from Papá, but if you hadn't run to him like a small tattle-tale child, you could have come to me and had a discussion."

He stopped pacing and stared her in the face. "Run to him, Rachel? Think about what you're saying! You left home, took Ana with you, and rode to the mission with no protection. You managed to get yourself captured by a drunken bandito and dragged into a cantina in Tubac. Don't you realize they could have killed you? And do you realize what else could have happened to you at the hands of Molina?"

Rachel twisted her hands. "Yes, Paulo. I fully

realize what could have happened to me." She squared her shoulders and glared at him. "And I also realize that there were two men who bravely stood up to Molina and his bandits. Rusty Cunningham and Father Antonio!" She raised her voice. "Where were you, Paulo? Rusty had already freed me from Molina before you ever showed up."

Paulo flinched at the insult. "Rachel, you go too far." His voice was a low growl. "Maybe you *deserve* to be the wife of an American cowboy who can never offer you anything but a one-room shack and a bunch of bawling babies."

Before she could think, she slapped his face. "He can offer me exactly what I want. Love, kindness, and gentleness. And one thing you'll never have—the ability to make my heart pound when he comes near." She softened her voice. "Paulo. I just don't love you."

He went still a moment, then shook his head. "You'd better learn to accept this marriage, Rachel. It has been approved by both our families. We've had our engagement fiesta. I will not break the traditions of many generations by rejecting the match our fathers made for us." He held his hands out. "Don't you know what a perfect match we are, Rachel?"

Before he could say another word, Teresa walked onto the patio, her eyes wide as saucers.

"Rachel, I could hear you shouting all the way in the foyer. What on earth is going on here?"

Paulo turned his back and walked to the fountain

without saying a word. Rachel took a deep breath and said, "We were discussing many things, Teresa. Nothing you need to concern yourself with."

Teresa frowned. "I came to tell you that Papá wants to see you. He'd like you to come to his study and speak with him."

Rachel leaned her head back and sighed deeply. "Yes, I'll go to him in one moment."

She watched as Teresa's eyes sought out Paulo, who stood with his back to them, arms crossed tight across his chest and his head down.

"What have you done to him, now?" Teresa kept her voice low. "Why does it seem that every time you two are together you upset him? Where is your heart?"

"My heart belongs to someone else, as you well know." She nodded to Paulo. "Go to him, Teresa. I must go to Papá."

~

Rachel tapped on the door of Papá's study. A weak, shaky voice uttered, "Come in." She entered slowly and crossed the short distance to his desk.

"Papá, Teresa said you wanted to see me."

Domingo leaned his head back on his chair. "Yes, mija, I haven't seen you since the episode with my heart yesterday." His speech was low and creaky. "Both my other daughters have visited with me, but not my Rachel."

She sat in the chair before his desk. "I'm sorry, Papá. I feel responsible for your episode, and I didn't want to upset you again." In her mind, a voice screamed, *Tell him, Rachel. You're going to be with Rusty and not Paulo. He needs to accept this simple fact.*

Papá reached across his desk and took her hand with a feeble grasp. "I understand, my dear. I am feeling a little better now."

Rachel pulled her hand back and looked down at her wrist. Her eyes fell on the silver bracelet Rusty had placed on her arm, and his voice echoed in her mind. *Yes, I love you. I'll love you till I draw my last breath...*

She stiffened her spine. "I have great respect for you, Papá, and I never want to cause you pain. But you must know by now how much I love Rusty and…"

Domingo groaned loudly and threw a hand to his chest. "Please bring me water." He dropped his head back and moaned. "My heart…my heart."

Rachel jumped to her feet and ran to the credenza, poured some water, and hurried back to his side. "Here, Papá." She held the glass to his lips.

"Thank you, my daughter." He looked up at her from under furrowed brows. He croaked. "What were you saying to me, dear girl?"

"Nothing, Papá. Nothing."

~

After the upsetting conversation with her father, Rachel retreated to her favorite place of solace—the shady patio. *Oh, how I wish Mamá were here. I need so much to talk to her.* Tía Maria's words drifted through her mind. She'd told Papá that Teresa would be the perfect match for Paulo because she truly loved him. But he'd refused to even listen.

Two muscular arms wrapped around her waist from behind. Rusty leaned down and nuzzled her shoulder, laying the softest of kisses on it.

"I couldn't wait any longer. I haven't been able to think about anything but you since we talked yesterday. How did your Papá take it when you told him about us?" When he spoke, his breath blew the curls at the nape of her neck, sending shivers down her spine.

Rachel turned to him and wrapped her arms around his neck. He kissed her face, then claimed her lips with a passion that promised things she dared not dream about. He pulled away from her, but she couldn't open her eyes. She'd waited for this kiss since being with him yesterday—fantasized about it a hundred times.

Rusty held her so close she could hear his heartbeat. He kissed the top of her head and whispered. "Hon, we could have our wedding here, then go back to Missouri until things settle down with your Papá. Or we can stay here in Sonora if that'll make you happy." His deep voice rumbled in her ear. He lifted her chin, his hazel eyes soft with love. "Just tell me what you want, darlin'."

A small, desperate sound escaped Rachel's lips. She backed up a step, threw a hand to her face, and turned toward the fountain.

Rusty froze. "Rachel?" He moved toward her and touched her shoulder. "What's happened?"

A shudder slid through her. She looked up at him and shook her head. "When I told Papá yesterday that I wouldn't marry Paulo, he had a terrible spell with his heart. Dr. Garcia said that another such shock could kill him." She looked up at him. "Even after that, I tried to discuss it with him again today and he had another episode."

She watched the play of emotion cross Rusty's face. His eyes, so gentle and hopeful only a moment ago, dimmed and became blank. His expression wilted like a flower in the desert heat. "What are you saying?" A cynical look crossed his eyes. "Oh. I understand." He backed away from her. "Hey, we both got caught up in our emotions yesterday. So many things happened—you being kidnapped from the mission and all the drama that took place in one short afternoon." Rusty laughed, but it was the saddest sound she'd ever heard. "We should probably just pretend all our talk of love and being together never took place."

Rachel ran to him and grabbed his hand. "Rusty, no! I'll pretend no such thing. Just give me a little more time to talk to Papá."

He pulled away from her. "Well, Rachel, it seems like time is the one thing we ain't got. You and Paulo are supposed to be having a wedding rehearsal tomorrow. I guess that'll go on as planned." He turned and strode toward the gate.

Rachel hurried to his side and grabbed his arm. "No, Rusty. I'll postpone the rehearsal. I'll find a way to make Papá understand."

"I just don't see how you could. It's looking like me and Jared are pullin' out of here tomorrow and starting for home." He whirled around and tramped through the gate.

"Rusty!" Rachel darted after him, but he was gone.

~

Rusty's head roared with shock and disbelief. His gut tied itself into a thousand painful knots. He couldn't think straight. Only an hour before, he'd thought Rachel would be his wife, and now he found himself crashing back to reality. He was just a cowboy with nothing but a horse to his name. *Well, that's okay. How did I really expect this to turn out?*

He stomped toward the corral and found Trueno, the mustang he'd been riding since sending his mount home with the herd. He stroked the horse's neck and Trueno nuzzled him. Rusty sucked in a deep breath and blew it out. "Tomorrow, my friend. I'll be gone tomorrow and I'll put this all behind me." He patted the horse's muscular shoulder. "I'm going back where I belong. I don't know what I was thinking, anyway. A country boy like me had no business ever falling for a girl like Rachel. I could never fit into her world." He stroked the mustang again and Trueno nickered. "Yeah, I was just dreaming. I'll get over her in time." The pain that clenched his heart told him otherwise.

A shout came from the direction of the great room. Paulo's angry voice boomed through the open door and Bonita's frightened, high-pitched pleas drifted in the air.

Rusty stormed toward the house, Paulo's shouts getting louder by the moment. Rusty burst into the room by way of the portico and found Bonita cowered near the door to the foyer, her eyes wide as Paulo raged.

"There you are, Cunningham." Paulo turned around slowly as Rusty entered the room. He pointed a finger at Rusty and took a step toward him. "I was just about to send this useless maid to find you."

Rusty spoke to the cringing woman. "You can go, ma'am. Sorry you got pulled into this." Bonita gave a small curtsy and sped from the room.

"Who do you think you are, Cunningham?" Paulo stood a head shorter than Rusty but he strode up and jammed a finger in his chest. His face reddened with anger. "Do you even realize what you have done to this family? What you've done to our community with your foolishness?" He slashed the air with his arms. "You ride in here to stay for a couple of weeks and drag my fiancée into your little game of romance. You've caused her to turn her back on everything and everyone she's ever known. Her Papá could have died because of the terrible shock Rachel gave him yesterday!" He blew out an exasperated breath. "And how will this all end? How many people will have been hurt when you ride away?"

Rusty felt pride surge up in his chest. He glared at Paulo with blood in his eye. "Delgado, I've had it with your rants and your threats." Paulo visibly shrank back as Rusty confronted him. "You have the gall to accuse me of hurting the Rios family by the simple act of loving Rachel when just a day ago you rode away when her life was in danger. You aren't man enough to protect the woman you intend to marry."

Paulo took a step closer. "Don't accuse me of failing to protect Rachel. You evidently made a deal with Benito that resulted in Carlos Rodriguez escaping. He is still on the loose, still rustling cattle—even though you blatantly accused me of being behind this." He snorted a laugh. "The very thought that you would accuse someone like me of stealing horses is laughable. Don't you know these ranches are my legacy? Why would I do something that would hurt the community of hacendados I belong to?"

Rusty inched even closer to Paulo. "From what I've seen, you don't give a thought to anyone's happiness but your own. More than once I've heard you yelling at Rachel and even poor Bonita. Don't you *ever* try to pretend I'd hurt Rachel. I'd lay my life down for that girl and I'd move heaven and earth to give her the good life she deserves."

Paulo sneered. "You say you wouldn't hurt her or her family but you are selfish enough to take Señor Rios's daughter from under his nose, causing him to die of a broken heart!"

"Yeah, I heard that her papá almost died yesterday. I'm sorry about that." His voice was low. "I have a lot of respect for the man."

"Yes, you fool!" He continued his tirade. "He could have died. And you have only yourself to thank for that." He shook his head. "Do you really think she'll be happy with you once she receives word that her Papá has died as a result of her selfish act? She'll leave you and your American life before a year is up."

Rusty narrowed his eyes at Paulo, then turned, and walked to the door, gazing into the day's last rays of sunlight. Rachel's distraught face flashed through his mind. He knew she loved him but Paulo was right. If her Papá died, guilt would crush their chance at happiness. In that moment he knew what he had to do. He let out a slow, resigned sigh and spoke without turning around. "Well, I reckon you can relax, Delgado. Me and my boss will be on our way back to Missouri tomorrow. And your wedding and your well-planned life can go on just as you arranged."

Chapter Fifteen

Rachel lay sobbing on her bed, her face buried in a pile of feather pillows. Why did this have to happen? How was she supposed to choose between the man she loved and her Papá's very life? There must be an answer. *Lord, please help me find a solution. I don't want to spend my life with Paulo, forever grieving the loss of Rusty.*

The shadows grew long in her bedroom, and she sat up on the bed. Rusty had said he was leaving in the morning. Tomorrow she'd stand with Paulo before a priest and practice her vow to be his faithful wife until death parted them. And Rusty would be boarding a stagecoach in Tucson to ride out of her life forever. *I must try one more time to stop him.*

Someone tapped on her door. She crossed the deeply shadowed room and opened it to find Bonita holding a tray of food.

"I'm sorry, I don't want anything right now. Take it away, please."

"Señorita, you must eat. You'll make yourself

sick."

Rachel wanted to say she was already sick but instead shook her head. "Take it back to the kitchen." She started to close the door, then opened it again. "Bonita. Please find Señor Cunningham and ask him to meet me on the patio. I must speak to him."

Bonita nodded. "Yes, ma'am."

Rachel took a pace back and something crinkled under her foot. She looked down to see an envelope with her name on it lying on the floor. Her heart skipped a beat as she picked it up and tore it open. Hands shaking, she lit a lamp and dropped into a chair.

My Darling Rachel,

I know what a terrible choice you've had to make. I know you love me. I can see it in your eyes when you look at me and feel it all the way to my soul when we kiss. I'll remember every look and every kiss until the day I die. But, Hon, neither one of us can be the cause of your papa's death. I'm taking the choice out of your hands. I'll be leaving here tonight.

I hope that once you're married, Paulo will settle down and let go of his anger. I figure I was the cause of it anyways. My sweetheart, I hope you learn to care for Paulo and have a house full of children to fill your life with joy.

Remember, I'll always love you.

Rusty

Rachel clasped the letter to her chest and ran to

the window. He was already gone.

She snatched the door open, then sped down the stairs and out to the back of the hacienda. "Pedro, have you seen Señors Cunningham and Gentry this evening?"

"Sí, they took a couple of horses and rode toward Tucson about an hour ago."

Rachel stared down the road Rusty and Jared would have ridden away on. Her heartbeat slowed to a dull, hollow, thud. She stumbled back into the house and returned to her bedroom. Rachel read his letter over and over again. Rusty had made the decision for them. Neither of them could risk being the cause of Papá's death.

She folded the letter and pressed it into her bodice. Tomorrow her life would change forever. Suddenly, she felt old, tired, and hopeless. She crawled into a chair and faced the window. If only she could see Rusty on the red dirt road…riding back to her.

~

The sun glared through Rachel's window, hot and oppressive across her face. She squinted her eyes open, then pulled her coverlet over her head. She didn't want to face this day. Maybe yesterday had all been only a bad dream.

A heavy knock sounded at her door. "Señorita, we have your bathtub."

Rachel sighed. Servants waited outside her door with the heavy bathtub and buckets of warm water. She crawled out of bed and slipped on her wrapper.

"Coming. One moment."

She opened the door and a parade of servants entered her room with the tub and water, followed by Bonita carrying a tray of food. A somber-looking Ana trailed behind the others.

"My goodness—I've barely opened my eyes!" Rachel watched as the servants filled her tub and Bonita set her breakfast on the dressing table.

"You have no time for lying in bed. You have your brunch at noon and the wedding rehearsal this afternoon." She crossed her arms and gave Rachel a stern look. "Eat. I will be back soon to help you dress."

Bonita left the room and Rachel sat down at the dressing table. She picked up her fork and speared a bite of melon. "I don't think I can get a morsel of food down." She rubbed her eyes. "I barely slept a wink last night."

Ana flopped into the white velvet chair next to the dressing table. "Señor Rusty left last night. I watched from my window as he and his friend rode away."

Rachel dropped her fork onto the tray. "I know, Ana. He slipped a letter under my door before he left."

Ana stepped over and wrapped her arms around Rachel's neck. "I'm sorry, my sister. I know you love him." Her voice lowered with sadness. "And now, you must marry the *idiota* Paulo."

Rachel sighed and hugged her tight. "Somehow I must find the strength to face this." She looked up at

Ana. "But now I need to take my bath and prepare for this day."

Ana left the room and Rachel slid into the tub of warm water. As she wriggled her toes, she looked down at her still swollen and sore ankle. All the activity of the past couple of days had made it worse. She hadn't stayed off her feet as she should have. She remembered Rusty carrying her to her room after her fall down the stairs. And she remembered the kiss—all the kisses they'd shared. No one would ever make her feel that way again. Somehow, she'd manage. She could live out her life in a loveless marriage. She wasn't the first and wouldn't be the last. She wondered what Rusty was doing right now. Tears rolled down her face and she realized she was crying.

Chapter Sixteen

Rusty sat on the edge of the hard hotel bed. He rubbed his hands over his face and gazed around the small dusty room. The gray light of dawn illuminated the dingy, barren space. It was perfect in its bleak emptiness. This was what his life would be from here on out. Drab, empty, and colorless.

He stood and paced to the window. The sun wasn't fully up, but the heat was already stifling. Nothing moved outside, not even the breeze. The stage for Kansas City wouldn't be coming through Tucson until tomorrow, so he and Jared planned to just lay low in one of the cool adobes in town today and stay out of the sun.

He stared out toward the south. She was back there—probably getting out of bed and putting on one of her pretty dresses. In just a few days, she'd be Mrs. Paulo Delgado. They'd say their vows and he'd take her home, up the stairs to their new bedroom, and—no— Rusty couldn't think about it. He couldn't bear the image.

Nothing really mattered now. Jared would head home tomorrow to his new ranch and his lovely wife. Rusty was heading home to…nothing. He'd adjust. His life would get back to normal in time. He blew out a heavy breath and ran his hand through his unruly hair. *Just get through one day at a time.*

~

Rachel plodded down the staircase like someone going to a funeral. The huge hacienda felt empty and hollow without Rusty's presence. She gathered up the skirt of the pale green satin dress she wore and headed toward the dining room. The voices of her family wafted out the door and reached her ears. Tía Maria spoke to Ana and Papá's booming voice shouted to someone. Rachel drifted into the room like a sleepwalker.

Papá sat at the head of the table enjoying his brunch before everyone would head to the chapel. "Rachel, mijita! Come in and sit with us. Today is a special day for you."

Rachel's head snapped toward him. "Yes, Papá…a very special day. There's never been another one like it for me."

Tía Maria looked up. "Rachel dear, you're as pale as a ghost. Are you ill?"

"I'm not feeling well, Tía. I didn't sleep much last night."

Papá furrowed his brow. "Get some food in your

stomach, Rachel. You have a full day ahead of you."

"Thank you, but no. I don't want any food." Rachel tried not to snap at her father, but the niggling feeling of resentment welled up inside her. She fought it down. It wasn't Papá's fault he had a weak heart. "I'll simply have a cup of tea and a sweet roll on the patio." She got her tea and roll from the buffet and strode through the door.

Teresa's voice reached her as she approached the fountain. Rachel stepped in the shadow of a potted palm and watched as Teresa stood over a seated Paulo. She had her hands on his shoulders and gently massaged them. "Paulo, I'm so sorry for the pain this has caused you. You don't deserve it. Any woman would be a fool to prefer another man over you." She gently stroked his wavy, black hair. "I'm sure everything will turn out okay. Once Rachel has separated herself from the Americano and become your wife, things will fall into place as they should."

Paulo reached up, took Teresa's hand, and kissed it. "Thank you, Teresa. Why can't Rachel be more like you?" He glanced up over his shoulder at her, with what could only be described as an adoring look.

Teresa stroked his hair again. "Someday you'll be a great hacendado like Papá and your father. You'll be one of the two or three supreme ranchers of Sonora." She kneaded his shoulders again. "And you deserve that position, Paulo. You were born to it."

Teresa seemed to suddenly become aware of

someone's presence and she lurched around. Shock must have shown clearly on Rachel's face. Teresa sighed, squared her shoulders, and walked past Rachel. She looked every bit as depressed and miserable as Rachel felt.

They were plainly in love with each other. This arranged marriage not only hurt her and Rusty but Teresa and Paulo, too. Teresa adored him. They had the same desires and goals for their lives. Anyone could see they were the perfect match.

Rachel went to Paulo and looked down at him. Discontent shone in his downcast eyes and his pouting mouth. "Paulo, I'm sorry I've made you so unhappy."

He looked up at her as though waking from a daydream. He sighed. "It doesn't matter, Rachel. Let's just get this day over with." He stood and strode into the dining room. *What a happy mood everyone is in for this "special day."*

~

Papá opened the ornately carved oak door of the family's private chapel and walked through. Tía Maria and the three Rios girls trailed behind, with Rachel straggling at the end of the line. The fun and anticipation she always imagined were nowhere to be found. The trek into the chapel held all the joy of going to a wake.

After Rachel sat at a small dressing table, Tía Maria stood behind her adjusting the curls in Rachel's hair. She set the comb on the dresser. "Where's your

Mamá's necklace? I'll fasten it for you."

"I think Papá was going to get it from the safe." Rachel stood and turned toward the door. "I'll go ask him about it." She headed for the back of the chapel where Papá and Dr. Garcia were talking together.

"And your health, Domingo. How are you feeling?" Dr. Garcia's voice lowered in concern.

"I believe I am much better, Eduardo. There was truly just one attack. After that, I may have exaggerated my condition a little—especially when Rachel came to me the second time." He shrugged and gave the doctor a sheepish smile. "She tried to tell me she wanted to end her engagement and marry the American cowboy. However, a man does what he must for his family." Domingo stopped talking as she approached and he and Dr. Garcia both turned sharply to her.

Rachel stopped in her tracks. He had exaggerated? Just how much had he dramatized his condition?

"Rachel, my dear!" Papá plastered a smile on his face. "What is it? I thought you were getting ready to begin the rehearsal."

"Yes, I am." She looked at the floor and tried to process the information she'd just learned. "I came to ask you if you remembered to bring Mamá's necklace for me."

"Ah, yes, I did." He reached into his breast pocket, retrieved a slender box, and handed it to her.

"Thank you, Papá." Rachel couldn't meet his eyes. She nodded curtly and ran back to the dressing room where Tía Maria waited for her.

Minutes later, Rachel stood at the back of the chapel, her arm linked through her father's, as an organist played. Emotions like stormy ocean waves pitched her in every direction. She didn't have time to sort through all the thoughts bombarding her. Rusty had ridden out of her life, Papá had shackled her to a man she didn't care for—a man she now realized her sister loved. And minutes ago, she'd learned Papá had exaggerated his heart condition.

As she approached the end of the aisle, she glanced at Paulo, who waited there. He stood, shoulders back with a self-satisfied smirk on his face. The expression slipped for a moment as he cast a glance at Teresa and an unmistakable look passed between them. "What if?"

Papá moved away from Rachel's side and joined her sisters. Her gaze drifted out the window, across vast open plains stretching beyond the estate. As Father Antonio guided the group through the ceremony, her heart pounded. A vibrant image emerged of the little ranch Rusty had talked about building someday. She pictured Rusty and herself sitting at their own dinner table, sipping coffee, and talking through the events of their day.

As the Padre droned on, Rachel's eyes drifted to Teresa. Her eyes misted as she gazed at Paulo—they seemed to tell him an unspoken goodbye. Rachel glanced at Tía Maria and Dr. Garcia. The love between them was evident. Though they'd never openly declared their love for each other, it was palpable when they were together.

Anxiety welled up in Rachel's chest and perspiration broke out on her face. Her eyes darted to the window again. No, she couldn't do it. She couldn't go through with this farce.

Rachel's legs buckled and her vision dimmed. The advantage of exaggerated illness made sense now. *Thank you, Papá.* She threw a hand to her forehead, then dropped to the floor.

"Rachel!" Tía Maria raced to her side. "Eduardo, come quickly. I think she has fainted."

"Yes, I'm sure the excitement and the heat of this building was too much for her." Dr. Garcia picked Rachel up and carried her to the rear of the chapel, as Paulo stood idly, staring down at her but making no move to help. Tía Maria and Ana followed behind while Dr. Garcia carried Rachel to a chair and took her pulse.

Maria gently patted her face. "Are you okay now, my dear?"

Papá hurried to her side. "How are you, mijita? You gave me a terrible fright."

Rachel sat up straighter. "Yes, I'll be fine. I think I became overheated." She pushed a stray lock of hair from her face. "Papá, go back to Paulo. I just need a few minutes to gather myself."

Domingo kissed Rachel on the cheek and started

back toward the front of the chapel.

Rachel stumbled to the door. She opened it and stood in the doorway, sucking in a deep breath of the desert air. Again, she gazed to the north—toward Tucson. Rusty would still be there. It would be so easy. One of the vaquero's horses stood saddled and tethered just outside the chapel. Now was the moment. The rest of her life was on the line. She turned back to Tía Maria.

"Forgive me for hurting you, Tía. I'm going to Rusty. I can't go through with this. Tell Papá I love him and tell Paulo I'm sorry." Tears streaked her face as she ran into Tía Maria's arms.

"Go, my sobrina. Go find your happiness." Maria held Rachel close, then pushed her back to arm's length. "You see me, my dear. I've lived my life without love until now." She gazed at Dr. Garcia. "Go to the man you love and live the life you dream about. Your Papá will be okay, and so will Paulo."

Rachel hugged her tighter and glanced over Maria's shoulder. Ana stood a few feet away. She twisted her small hands, then wiped tears away with her palm. Ana's anguished face tore at Rachel's heart.

"Come here, sweet girl." Rachel held out a hand. Ana ran to her, and Rachel pulled her into the hug with Tía Maria.

A sob wracked Ana and she choked out her words. "You're leaving, Rachel."

"I swear I'll be back—I won't be gone forever.

Don't cry, my baby sister…you'll see me again soon, I promise."

She kissed Maria and Ana, then looked back toward her father, who sat on a pew facing the altar. Teresa stood before Paulo with a hand on his cheek. Rachel knew that his unhappiness at her leaving would be short-lived, with Teresa offering her special attention.

With a last look at her loved ones and a nod to Dr. Garcia, Rachel turned and ran out the door. She pulled up her skirt and mounted the horse that stood outside the chapel. "Quiet, girl." The mare made no sound as it walked to the end of the drive where Rachel kicked its sides. They raced onto the road leading off the Rios Rancho at a dead run.

~

The sun hung low on the horizon. Soon she'd be traveling by only whatever light the night sky offered. It would be a long, hard ride, and the dangers she faced were many. Banditos trekked the road between the Mexican border and Tucson. Her horse could step into a hole in the darkness, hurting itself and her. Worse, she had no water with her on this journey of several hours.

Rachel glanced over her shoulder, expecting to see a rider gaining on her. By now, Papá and Paulo must realize she was gone. Her heart pounded wildly in her chest. She could only hope that Tía Maria had come up with a story to buy her some time.

After what seemed like thirty minutes of hard

riding, Rachel slowed her horse to a trot. Her carefully styled hair now blew behind her in loose, wild strands. She felt grit on her damp face. Every sound in the gathering darkness seemed magnified a hundred times. Noises she hadn't heard during her hard run from the chapel assaulted her ears. Hoofbeats thudded in the desert behind her, or was it only her imagination? Simply the sounds of the night, or did a band of renegade Apaches trail her? What predatory beasts crouched in wait at the side of the road?

Rachel noticed a canteen hanging from the pommel of her saddle and opened it. Barely a quarter of the way full. She took a small swallow and replaced the cap.

It was fully dark now and the air took on a chill. A coyote howled somewhere in the dark desert.

Heavenly Father, please send Your angels to ride with me.

Despite the dangers, she was going and nothing could stop her.

~

Rusty and Jared scraped back chairs at their table in the café. Rusty moved slower than an old man as he dropped into his seat. He ran a hand down his face, scratching the two days' worth of stubble he hadn't bothered to shave. Miserable as an abandoned puppy, he rubbed tired eyes.

On the other hand, Jared's face glowed with happiness—he'd soon be on his way home to his wife and little ranch in Missouri. When he got there, his lovely Evangeline and precious herd of horses would be waiting for him.

"The dinner special looks good to me." Jared whistled some happy tune and unfolded his napkin. "What are you having?" He looked from the chalkboard menu on the wall to his friend's face.

Rusty mumbled something under his breath and slouched down in his chair.

Jared cocked an eyebrow. "Are you sure you really want to go back with me? I heard Rachel tell you she didn't want you to leave. Don't let your pride get in the way of your happiness."

"My pride's got nothin' to do with it. There're a dozen other reasons I needed to walk away from her." He laced his fingers on the table in front of himself. "I told you her Papá almost died right in front of her when she told him about us."

Jared shook his head and looked at him with skeptical eyes. "Rusty...buddy. Not to be cold-hearted but she can't live her life to please 'Papá.' He's a nice man and I'll be forever grateful for the help he gave me, but he's got two other daughters he could marry off to Delgado."

Rusty stared out the window, then shook his head. "Nope. I can't do it. If he dropped dead, Rachel would blame herself. And she'd end up blaming me, too." He scowled at Jared. "And by the way, do you have to be so danged cheerful? You're giving me a headache."

He looked up when the waitress came to their table and poured coffee for them. She took their orders, then left.

Jared folded his arms, tipped back his chair, and rocked. "Well, I know it's a letdown, but you'll be over her in a month, anyway." He gave Rusty a sideways glance. "These things happen when a man's on the trail. Some young gal comes along with stars in her eyes— thinks she's in love with you. Yep, it's happened before and I'm sure it'll happen again."

Rusty whipped his head around and stared at Jared like he'd lost his mind. "Rachel isn't just some *gal* with stars in her eyes." Heat climbed up his neck.

Jared set his chair flat on the floor and started drumming his fingers on the table. "I'm hungry. Where's that food?"

"And you know, I've had a few chances with other girls. It ain't like I couldn't find another girl if I wanted to." Rusty blew out a frustrated breath.

"Oh, I know…I know. It's just that I've learned from experience that a man can meet a girl—even a sweet, beautiful, Christian girl who claims to be head-over-heels in love with him, and once he's home, that pretty face will fade fast. Soon you won't even be able to remember her name." Jared crossed his ankle over his other knee. "Yeah…let Paulo Delgado have the woman you love…I suppose he deserves that special favor." He cocked an eyebrow at Rusty.

"Jared Gentry, if you weren't my best friend and

boss, I'd bust you a good one in the jaw right about now."

Jared laughed and shrugged. "Why? I'm just agreeing with you."

Rusty rubbed his hands over his face. "No, I ain't letting you do this to me. I made a decision to do what's best for everyone and I can't turn back on it now."

The waitress set their plates in front of them and refilled their cups.

"Okay. You know your own mind." Jared dug into his steak and roasted potato.

Rusty scooted his food around on his plate and then shoved it away.

He pushed back from the table. "I'm gonna go stretch my legs—maybe check on the horses and arrange to get them back to the Rios ranch."

The clomp of his heavy footsteps echoed on the wooden boardwalk. As he made his way further down Main Street, the raucous sounds of Tucson coming to life assaulted his ears. It was Saturday night and rowdy cowboys and vaqueros looking for a good time bustled through the streets.

Rusty stepped off the sidewalk and dodged a wagon as he crossed to the other side of the road. In front of the barbershop, a young family climbed into their buggy. The man swooped his little curly-haired boy down from his shoulders and handed him to a pretty, smiling Mamá who waited on the vehicle's seat. They were probably about to head home to their own cottage somewhere nearby. To hearth and home. Rachel's face flashed through his mind. What would their child look like?

He strode toward the livery where the horses were stabled, his gait getting faster as his agitation grew. He mumbled to himself. "Cunningham, you're ten kinds of a fool. You'll never find another girl like Rachel."

Rusty stopped in his tracks and dropped onto a wooden bench in front of the General Store. He clasped his hands together and leaned forward, staring down at the dusty boardwalk. Jared was right. *Rachel's in my blood, I can't let her go without a fight. I'm going back for her before that wedding to Delgado takes place. That little banty rooster couldn't make her happy…he only wanted the Rios wealth.*

Shouts and whoops grew louder as the town filled with revelers. Uncertainty plagued him as he argued with himself. *No, she wouldn't be happy on a little ranch in Missouri. She's grown up in wealth and privilege.*

He shook his head and rubbed a hand over his weary eyes. But Rachel was a different kind of woman than her sister. Teresa would make a better matron over the Rios estate.

Rusty stood and took a few faltering steps toward the livery stable. If he went back for Rachel, would he make a complete fool of himself? She might have changed her mind. She might reject him and tell him to go away and never come back.

He took a deep breath and ran a hand through his wild hair. "I'm going back. If I don't, I'll always wonder what might have been."

Chapter Seventeen

Rachel slumped forward over her saddle. Her eyelids drooped, then snapped open again as she fought to stay awake. Her back and legs ached from hours in the saddle, and she shivered in the cool night air. How much further to Tucson? She scanned the long, dark road ahead and the shadowed desert beside her. Had she drifted off to sleep and her horse turned onto a wrong trail?

She removed the cap from her canteen and took a sip of water. There were only a few swallows left.

A noise drifted to her again. The thud of hoof falls in the distance behind her. No, it wasn't a figment of her imagination, but it made no sense. Why hadn't whoever followed her caught up by now and done whatever horrors they had planned for her?

Rachel gazed up at the star-strewn sky and prayed. *Lord, please help. I think someone is following me and I'm not even sure I'm going the right way.*

Her horse snorted and instinctively picked up its pace. Rachel's eyes followed the dusty road to the horizon. In the distance, she saw a warm, ambient glow of light over a town. *Tucson!* She patted the mare's neck and urged her on, both horse and rider suddenly energized. "We must be getting close, girl."

Rachel rode into Tucson on Main Street, her heart in her throat. Jangling piano music, laughter, and loud voices drifted from the saloon. The aroma of seared steak drifted from a nearby café. Her stomach growled and reminded her that all she'd had to eat today was a sweet roll and a cup of tea. She was exhausted, hungry, and grimy, but she was here at last.

Where was Rusty and Jared's hotel? Her horse directed itself to the trough in front of the saloon and she allowed it a small drink of the cool water. As Rachel pulled her hair back into a loose twist, she scanned the street for a building that looked like it might be the hotel.

The saloon doors burst open, and a drunk staggered into the street. "Well, well, well…what have we here? *Como estas, señorita?* Come down here and talk to me." He stumbled up to the side of Rachel's horse and grabbed her arm. Rachel shied away from him, put a foot into his chest, and shoved him back.

He looked up and horror filled Rachel's mind. "Carlos Rodriguez!"

He grabbed her arm again.

"What are you doing? Did you follow me here?" She whipped at him with the reins of her horse. "Leave me alone, you're drunk."

He laughed and tugged harder on her arm. "Well, what a coincidence. If it isn't the princess of Rancho del Rios in the flesh."

A horse bounded up behind her and a rider leapt to the ground. "Señorita! Are you okay?"

Rachel whirled around to see a familiar figure grab the front of Carlos' shirt. "Pedro?"

Pedro sent the drunken Rodriguez sprawling back into the water trough. He reached up and steadied Rachel's skittish mare. "Yes, señorita. Your Tía Maria sent me behind you to make sure you got here safely."

She squeezed his hand. "So, it was you I heard behind me in the desert?" She laughed softly. "Well, as grateful as I am to see you, I wish I'd known it was a friend following me for the past several hours."

"I'm sorry…I only attempted to keep my distance as Señora Rios instructed."

Before he could say another word, Carlos rebounded, came up behind him and plowed into Pedro. They exchanged punches and Pedro took a vicious right hook to his chin. Rachel screamed, "Pedro!" She jumped down from her horse and ran to his side.

~

Rusty rounded the corner of the livery stable. As much as he dreaded hearing Jared say, "I told you so," he was about to tell his friend he'd been right. Yes, he was going back to the Rios ranch to claim Rachel as his own. What would happen from there? Only heaven knew.

As he paced down the dimly lit street, a female voice rang out and made his blood run cold. He stopped in his tracks and listened. The voice said, "Pedro! Are you okay? No…leave me alone!"

Drunken shouts and laughter followed the girl's distressed cries.

Rusty ran forward a few feet and strained to see what was happening down the road. A girl struggled in front of the saloon, her long black hair falling loose behind her as she fought against a rowdy reveler. "Rachel?" No, it couldn't be. She thrashed and kicked as the drunk man-handled her.

"Rachel!" Rusty shouted at the top of his lungs.

She turned and looked at him, terror registering on her face. Amazement coursed through him, but yes, it was Rachel grappling with an oddly familiar-looking drunk in front of the saloon. He raced toward her just as she broke free and made a dash for him.

Rachel ran only a few feet when her sprained ankle gave out and sent her sprawling onto the dusty road.

The furious man snarled and stumbled after her. "No woman treats me like that. Who do you think you are?" He grabbed her by her arm and dragged her back toward the saloon through the dirt.

Rusty reached the man, doubled his fist, and sent him careening back onto the boardwalk. In the moment between throwing his punch and it connecting, he recognized the face of Carlos Rodriguez. Momentarily in shock, Rusty looked from Rodriguez to Rachel, then to Pedro who was now lifting himself off the ground.

Rusty turned back to Rachel and fell on his knees beside her. "Dear Lord, Rachel. I can't believe you're really here." He scooped her into his arms, held her back, and stared into her face. "What are you all doing? What's going on?" He crushed her to his chest and planted a kiss on the top of her head.

"You aren't leaving here without me." She gazed up into his face, her eyes determined.

Rusty didn't know whether to laugh or cry. He decided to laugh. "Is that so?" He took her hands in his and helped her to her feet.

Behind him, the sheriff hustled across the street as fast as his older legs would take him. He rushed up beside Rodriguez and flipped him onto his back by the hair of his head. He turned to Rachel. "Somebody told me this man was assaulting you."

"Yes, Sheriff, that is correct. And he also struck my friend, Pedro, who was defending me."

"Don't worry, ma'am. I'll get him locked up if I can find an empty spot to shove him into on a Saturday night."

Rachel took an uncertain step, wobbled, and almost fell again.

Rusty swooped her up and started for the hotel, Pedro hobbling behind. "Let's get you out of the street and you can tell me all about it." He shook his head in bewilderment. "I still can't believe you rode all this way alone in the dark."

Inside the hotel lobby, Rusty deposited Rachel onto the round, tufted sofa and finally took a good look at her. Her green satin dress, torn and filthy, her hair a tangled mess. She threw a hand to her face and rubbed her cheek. "I must look like a street beggar."

"You look more beautiful than I've ever seen you." Rusty took her hand and kissed it.

Pedro limped in and sat down next to Rachel. He held a very sore-looking jaw.

"Are you okay? I'll go find the doc," Rusty said.

"No, no, please. I'm fine. My job here is done." Pedro looked at Rachel. "I was sent to protect Señorita Rios, and she is here now, safe and sound. I'll get some rest and head back to Nogales in the morning."

Rusty nodded. "Okay, if you're sure." He glanced at Rachel, then back to Pedro. "And I'm in your debt for taking care of this lady while she made that long ride. I'm mighty glad her aunt thought to send you along."

Rachel's stomach growled loudly, and she grabbed her middle. "I'm sorry. I haven't eaten all day."

Rusty took her hand and tugged her up off the sofa. "Come on, both of you. I'm taking you to the diner before you pass out from hunger."

Rachel looked toward the staircase. "What about Senor Gentry? He's here, isn't he?"

"I left him sound asleep a while ago. He still ain't

as strong as he thinks he is." Rusty shrugged.

"But I can't go into a restaurant looking like this!" Rachel pushed her unruly hair back from her face.

"Sweetheart, this is Tucson. No matter how much dust you have on your dress, you'll still be the best-looking girl to ever pass through the doorway of that diner. Now come on." He tugged her toward the exit. "Come on, Pedro." Rusty smiled. "Suddenly, I'm hungry, too."

After one more attempt at pulling her hair into a twist at the nape of her neck, Rachel followed Rusty and Pedro into the café. They found a seat in the corner and ordered steaks and all the trimmings. Rusty remembered how just a few hours earlier, he'd been here with Jared, miserable, exhausted from lack of sleep, and unable to eat a bite. My, how things had changed.

He looked across the table at Rachel. She blushed and looked down, the jade necklace at her throat catching the light. Rusty reached across the table and took her small hand.

"What happened, Rachel? I know you had your wedding rehearsal today."

She shrugged a shoulder. "I couldn't go through with it. I stood before Father Antonio with Paulo at my side, and all I could think about was you." She gazed at him, her eyes misty. "I heard your voice as you told me about a ranch in Missouri with blue-green hills and horses grazing in a meadow. That's what I want, Rusty.

Not the meaningless existence Paulo could have offered me."

Pedro coughed. Rachel looked at him, and he wiped a tear from the corner of his eye.

"I'm sorry, Pedro. I'm sure you didn't want to hear all this."

"No, señorita. I wish you and Señor Rusty good luck and happiness in your new life together."

Their food came, and the waiter lit a candle in the middle of their table.

After eating every morsel, Rachel sighed and pushed her plate back. "I must have looked like someone who hadn't eaten in a week."

Rusty laughed. "No, hon. I figure we jusst had our own private little engagement dinner. Just you, me, and Pedro."

Pedro lifted his cup and toasted the happy couple with a steaming mug of coffee.

Rusty paid the waiter and pulled back Rachel's chair. "We'd better go get rooms for you both at the hotel. It's getting a bit late and I know you're worn out."

From outside the diner door, angry shouts rang out. The door slammed back against the wall, and Paulo Delgado stepped into the café.

Chapter Eighteen

Rachel sat motionless, her eyes wide and her mouth agape.

Paulo stood with his fists balled at his sides. His eyes latched onto hers, burning with anger as if he'd been kindling it with every mile he rode to Tucson. "Get over here, Rachel. You're coming with me."

Rusty took Rachel by the arm and pulled her behind his back.

Pedro stepped aside, his eyes darting from Paulo to Rusty.

"Delgado. Surely you must know that there ain't no way on God's green earth that I'm gonna let you take Rachel back with you." Although there was no humor in Rusty's eyes, he let out a small chuckle. "If it's a fight you came here looking for, you've got it. I'll whip you any way you choose…fists, guns in the street. Name your pleasure."

The owner of the diner strode out of the kitchen. "Look, I'm not having any trouble here in my place. If you want to brawl, do it in the street."

"There won't be any trouble, Señor." Rachel stepped up beside Rusty. He attempted to push her behind him again, but she grabbed hold of his arm and stayed put.

Rachel's eyes implored him. "Paulo, this is just pride," she said. "Please admit it—at least to yourself if not to everyone else."

"Pride?" Paulo spewed the word at her. "You are my betrothed. You belong to me, Rachel!"

"I am *not* yours and I never belonged to you." Her eyes burned into his. "You have someone waiting for you at Rancho del Rios who loves you the way I love Rusty. Someone much more suitable for the life and future you want. I've seen you two together. I know you care for her, too. Why let silly pride stand between you and true happiness?" She shook her head at him. "I assure you I won't let you do this to me."

Paulo stood still as a statue and stared blankly across the room. "Teresa? Yes, she is a wonderful girl. She knows how to support and comfort a man. She'd make a perfect wife."

"Then you must know how her heart breaks at the thought of you and me marrying," she said.

A familiar voice spoke softly from across the room. "You are right, my daughter. Can you forgive a foolish old man?"

Rachel turned to see the sturdy figure of her father standing in the doorway, his body framed by the glow of lantern light.

"Papá! I can't believe you're here."

He held out his arms and she ran to him. "Did you mean that? Has your heart truly changed?" She gazed up into his face.

Papá sighed. "Yes, Rachel. Every word you said to Paulo is equally true of me. My pride has prevented me from allowing Teresa to be with the man she loves, just as I've kept you from seeking your happiness." He offered her a bittersweet smile. "My sister explained many things to me after you left today. I'm a stubborn man. I found it hard to admit the mistakes I'd made." He glanced at Paulo. "After you ran away today, in his anger, Paulo saddled up to track you down and I followed."

Rachel beamed up at him. "Whatever the reason, I'm glad you're here, Papá." She held out a hand to Rusty and he moved to her side. "Rusty and I are to be married tomorrow. Will you walk me down the aisle here in Tucson and give me away, as you'd planned to do at home?"

Paulo flinched and turned away.

Rachel turned to him again. "Please, Paulo. Won't you try to be happy? If only you'd believe and accept that you hold a world of happiness in your hands. Embrace it joyfully. Don't throw it away."

Paulo stole a glance at her. He sighed and shrugged. "Yes, Rachel. You're right. And strangely, I feel that you and Domingo have given me permission to admit my feelings for Teresa. I suppose we've both felt it for some time now but I couldn't admit it."

"Go to her. The arrangements are all in place for a beautiful wedding. Teresa needs only to step into the gown and the happiness she deserves."

"But surely you and Rusty will want to come back and have your wedding at the rancho." Papá's forehead wrinkled with displeasure.

The moment she'd been dreading was finally here. She leaned her head on his shoulder. "Forgive me for hurting you, but I'm going to Missouri with Rusty. That's where our ranch will someday be—our home we'll build together."

A look of devastation crossed his face, and he blew out a long, resigned breath. "Yes…I suppose I knew this to be true, but I held out some hope you'd come back to Sonora." He looked at Rusty. "I expected no less from Señor Cunningham, and in truth, I'd have been a little disappointed if he'd done anything differently. My father left Spain and brought his young bride with him to this new land."

Rusty extended his hand. "I can't tell you how happy it makes me to hear you say that. And don't you think it's time you called me Rusty?"

"And you can call me Domingo…or Papá if you wish." He shook Rusty's hand.

"I reckon Domingo'll do fine." Rusty curled his lips into a smile.

Paulo huffed at the scene taking place before him.

"I am going to the hotel to see if I can get myself a bed." He jerked his chin toward Pedro, who had retreated to the dinner table to watch the drama unfold. "Pedro, you can share a room with me and we can start for home at first light tomorrow."

"Thank you, but no. I am going to stay and watch Señorita Rios get married—especially now that I know her Papá will be a part of the wedding."

"Do as you please, but I'm leaving at sunrise." Paulo took a few steps toward the door. "I seem to be somehow motivated to get back to Rancho del Rios as quickly as I can tomorrow." He strode out the door.

~

Rusty strode down the quiet boardwalk. Tucson had finally gone to sleep. He rolled up the sleeves of his faded blue chambray shirt against the oppressive Arizona heat that hovered even at night.

He opened the door to Sheriff Johnson's jail. The lantern on his desk cast long shadows against the wall. The sheriff looked up, eyes wide with surprise. "Mr. Cunningham. I was hoping to see you. Looks like young Rodriguez had a bounty on him." He nodded to the row of cells lining the far wall.

Rusty cleared his throat. "Keep it, Sheriff. I didn't do it for any money." He shook his head. "He was attacking Rachel and I'd never stand by and let that happen." He looked down at the floor. "I was hoping, though, for a chance to speak with him. I have some questions I sure hope he can answer."

A small smile tugged at the older man's face. "Yeah, go on then."

Rusty felt his shoulders stiffen as he crossed the room toward Rodriguez. He leaned against the metal bars and peered into the shadows of the tiny cell. Carlos sat against the brick wall on a hard bench. He stared away from Rusty, curled in on himself.

Rusty took a breath in through his nose. "Rodriguez?"

Carlos' eyes darted to Rusty then away. His voice came out thin and quiet. "What?"

"Nah, you don't get to give me that. You've caused a lot of trouble recently. Hurt Rachel, got Jared shot even if you weren't the one pulled the trigger. I've spent a lot of time with my thoughts spinning in circles, wondering about it. This thing with the horse rustling has been eating me up since I got here." One hand wrapped around the bars of Rodriguez's cell. "Why'd you do it? Since the beginning, I've thought it was Delgado, but he was right. He said he had no reason to steal horses and, come to think of it, neither do you. Your papá is a big name hacendado with land and money. So, what made you think you needed to go off and start stealing these horses?"

Carlos turned to face Rusty, a low fire burning in his eyes. The turn of his mouth was sad, though, resigned. "You wouldn't understand, Cunningham. People like Paulo Delgado and a couple of others in the valley have their futures handed to them on silver platters. The oldest sons, they get the land, the horses, the prettiest girls. A golden life. The youngest son, like me—we're used as little more than cow hands. Used for hard work but with nothing to look forward to." His eyes glazed, unfocused. "I decided to create a future for myself, cutting myself a herd of horses, and getting a head start." His head snapped to the side, a harsh motion. "Yes, and now, thanks to you, my future is a few sad hours in a concrete cage, then a long walk…and a short drop."

Rusty's throat went dry. "You made that decision, Carlos. Didn't no one make you do it."

Carlos continued to stare at the wall. Rusty tugged at his sleeves again, nodded to Sheriff Johnson, and headed back to the hotel.

~

Rachel blinked against the early morning Arizona sun that blazed through the window of Sheriff Johnson's office. He took off his weathered hat and pulled on his black Justice of the Peace robe.

She and Rusty stood before him while she smoothed the skirt of her new white dress she'd bought at the mercantile. She touched her mother's jade necklace at her throat.

Rusty turned to Jared at his right hand and gave him a tense, nervous-looking grin. Papá shifted impatiently from foot to foot.

"Where's Pedro? He was supposed to be here with you, Papá." Rachel turned to the door for the third time.

"I don't know. He said he'd be right behind me." Papá ran a finger around his tight collar.

"Well, we must get started soon." Sheriff Johnson opened his Bible to the correct page. "I've got a hanging to officiate later this morning."

Rusty covered a gasp with a cough.

Rachel's eyes darted from Rusty to Papá. "I don't want to start without Pedro. He stayed in town especially for my wedding."

The door popped open and Pedro scuttled in. "Sorry I'm late, Señorita. It took me a while to find these for you." He held out a scraggly bouquet of Indian Blanket and Desert Marigold.

"Thank you, Pedro. These are beautiful." She clutched them to her chest and spun back to Sheriff Johnson as Pedro took his place beside her papá.

She turned and smiled up at Rusty then took his hand.

"Dearly beloved, we are gathered here today in the sight of God and these witnesses…"

The words of the ceremony floated past Rachel's ears, etching themselves into her heart for eternity. A mere few minutes later, she heard Rusty say, "I do," and he slipped a gold band on her finger.

As they stood at the Sheriff's desk signing their certificate, the door slammed open. "Better hurry! The stage is here and loading up."

Jared looked up at the man who stood in the

doorway. "We'll be right there. Don't let'em leave without us." He raced out the door to begin loading their meager possessions onto the coach's roof.

Papá and Pedro followed them to the stage. Rusty opened the door and turned to Rachel. "Are you ready, Mrs. Cunningham?"

She nodded, momentarily lost in his hazel eyes. "Yes, my husband. I'm ready."

She turned to her father, the tears already beginning to flow. She threw her arms around him. "Papá, I love you so much and I'm so happy you were with me today."

He choked on his words. "I love you, too, my sweet daughter. Never, never doubt that. And please know that everything I did was because I wanted to give you a good future."

"I believe you, Papá. And I'll see you again before long. Rusty has promised we'll be back to visit. Give everyone at home my love."

He pulled her into a fierce embrace and kissed her cheek.

She turned to Pedro. "Thank you for being a part of my wedding and for the beautiful flowers."

"You are welcome, Señorita…I mean, Señora." They all laughed.

Rusty helped his wife into the stagecoach and closed the door behind them.

Papá and Pedro saddled up and grabbed the leads to the extra horses going back with them. Domingo straightened his back, squared his shoulders, and slowly started toward home.

Rachel couldn't help it. She took one last look as the stage jolted forward. Out the window, she watched Papá and Pedro's backs as they rode down the red, dusty road toward Nogales. A tear streamed down her face as she thought of all she was leaving behind—her loving family, the Mission, the home she grew up in—all that was familiar in her life.

Rusty wrapped his arm around her and held her close to his side. She gazed into his kind, loving face, and thought about all that lay ahead. Someday, she and Rusty would sit on the porch of their home and gaze across the blue hills of their Missouri ranch.

As they rolled across Arizona territory, she remembered all she and Rusty had overcome to be together. It gave her the confidence to believe they could overcome any problems that came their way.

She snuggled under Rusty's arm and looked again out the window of the stage. As she gazed to the north and her bright future, she smiled.

Rusty beamed down at her. "We're on our way home, darlin'."

They had a long, long ride ahead of them, but they'd make it. They were together.

THE END

If you liked this book…

You can check out my previous novel, *The Gamble on Love*.

You can follow me and get a free short story at my website, ReginaRodgers.com

Amazon author page
Facebook page
or Instagram.

And please, **please do me the favor of writing a review** for the book on Amazon, Goodreads, and/or Bookbub!